INFUSION

INFUSION

Allan Cho   JF Garrard

Sophie Munk

Asian Canadian Writers Workshop publishes Ricepaper Magazine year round online. Visit Ricepapermagazine.ca for more details.

For permission requests, in correspondence, please send to "Attention: Editor-in-Chief," at the address below.

Ricepaper Magazine PO Box 74174 Centre Point Mall PO Vancouver, BC V5T 4E7

Alternatively: info@ricepapermagazine.ca www.ricepapermagazine.ca

First Edition

Library and Archives Canada Cataloguing in Publication

Title: Infusion / Allan Cho, JF Garrard, Sophie Munk.
Other titles: Infusion (2025)
Names: Cho, Allan, editor. | Garrard, J. F., 1978- editor.
Description: First edition. | Series statement: Ricepaper magazine books ; 4 Identifiers: Canadiana (print) 20240529375 | Canadiana (ebook) 2024053512X | ISBN 9781988416465 (softcover) | ISBN 9781988416472 (Kindle)
Subjects: CSH: Short stories, Canadian (English) | CSH: Canadian fiction (English)—21st century. | CSH: Canadian poetry (English)—21st century. | CSH: Canadian literature (English)—Asian Canadian authors. | LCGFT: Short stories. | LCGFT: Poetry.
Classification: LCC PS8235.A8 I54 2025 | DDC C810.8/08950710905—dc23

For our families

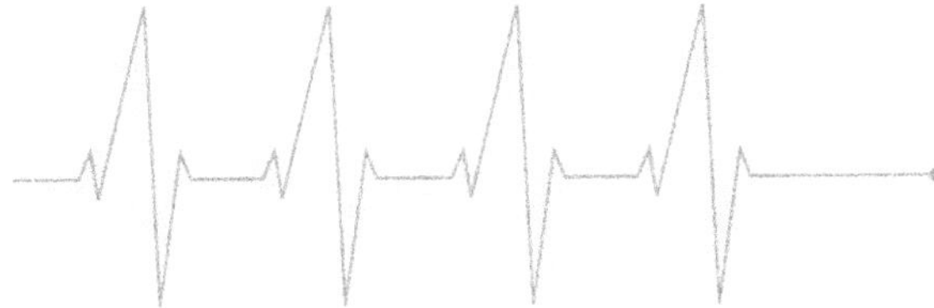

Ricepaper Magazine Titles

Ricepaper Magazine Books

Belief

Immersion: An Asian Anthology of Love, Fantasy, and Speculative Fiction

Currents: A Ricepaper Anthology

The Seven Muses of Harry Salcedo by Vincent Ternida

Ricepaper Magazine (online)

ricepapermagazine.ca

CONTENTS

Editors' Introduction

In the sprawling canvas of the Asian diaspora, a story of migration, adaptation, and cultural infusion unfolds. Across continents and oceans, millions of individuals have ventured far from their homelands, weaving their traditions, hopes, and aspirations into the diverse tapestry of the world. "Infusion" is a collection of stories that explores the vibrant and evolving experiences of the Asian diaspora, focusing on the narratives of immigration, the challenges faced by first-generation Asians, and the profound impact of generational changes.

In the heart of this anthology lies the theme of "infusion"—the delicate blend of cultures, beliefs, and identities that occurs when individuals from diverse backgrounds come together in a foreign land. As we delve into these tales, we embark on a journey that spans continents and generations, capturing the essence of the first-generation Asians who have made foreign lands their homes.

These stories are windows into the lives of those who have crossed borders and oceans, seeking refuge, opportunities, and a place to call their own. We witness the challenges faced by different characters as they navigate the delicate balance between preserving their cultural heritage and embracing the customs of their new homes. The clash of traditions and modernity, the yearning for a sense of belonging, and the resilience in the face of adversity—these are the themes that echo through the narratives of the diaspora.

In "The Southpaw," you'll meet a young man trying to understand the relationship between one's appearance and the country of one's birth. "Two Tins of Dried Smelts" explores the memories of an annual smelt run event in Parry Sound and a difficult childhood after the passing of a mother. The flowing poem "The Perpetual Foreigner" speaks of the constant question of a person's identity under constant scrutiny in their adopted land. "I'm Jealous of the Students at Seoul International" explores the emotional journey of immigrants trying to understand where they fit as they embrace new beginnings in foreign soil.

With each story, we explore the intricacies of cultural infusion—the amalgamation of languages, cuisines, and traditions that enrich the lives of those in the diaspora. The tales within these pages celebrate the resilience of the human spirit, the power of adaptation, and the beauty that arises when diverse cultures intertwine, creating a mosaic that is as intricate as it is harmonious.

As you read through these stories, may you feel the pulse of the diaspora—the heartbeat of generations striving to bridge the gap between the past and the present. "Infusion" invites you to embark on a poignant exploration of cultural infusion, where the stories of immigrants, their children, and their grandchildren converge to paint a vivid picture of the enduring spirit of the Asian diaspora.

FICTION

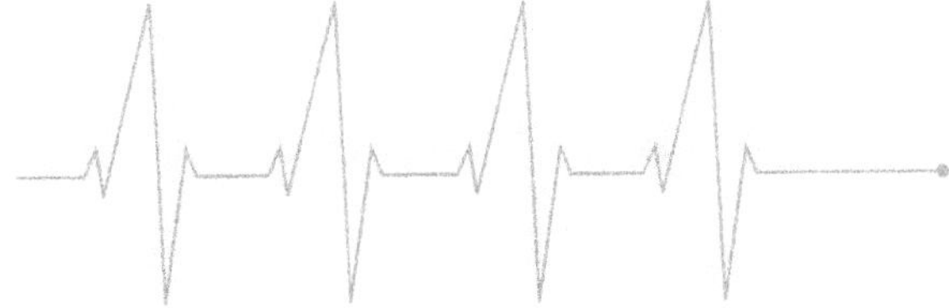

THE SOUTHPAW
BY KENNETH TANEMURA

An was staying in the home of a distant relation for the summer as his family's lease on their apartment had expired, and his mother had yet to receive the papers she needed to move the family to Canada. An was proud of his mother for becoming a full-time assistant professor of applied linguistics at the university, and he was grateful for his distant relations for taking them in. He was even happy his stepfather, John Fujima, found an adjunct teaching position as a basic writing instructor at the same university, so the family could stay together.

The home of An's new hosts was nestled in a quiet cul-de-sac.

"An, what are you doing? Eat with your right hand," Mr. Dung said. Mr. Dung was the distant relation who owned the house. He was 62. An, a southpaw since birth, shifted his chopsticks into his right hand and fumbled through the sliced pork and spinach.

"Is that a cultural thing?" An said. He was born in Vietnam but brought to America for kindergarten.

"Do as he says," said his mother, Ha.

"*Can* you do it?" John said.

"I'll try," An said. An looked up to John because he was an Asian born in America, a native speaker of English, though he wondered at how a man who looks Japanese could not speak Japanese or understand much about their culture.

"Eat like a gentleman," Mr. Dung said. "Like John. He Japanese, so he eat right."

"Except that he's not Japanese," An said.

"No, he Japanese," Mr. Dung said.

"He's an American," An said.

"He Japanese," Mr. Dung said.

"My father served in the US Army. No one's more American than the son of a man who served our country." John felt his patience being pulled at like an old, frayed rubber band. "Pour me another glass of wine, Mr. Dung," John said. Mr. Dung, a light drinker at best, widened his eyes.

Mr. Dung leaned close to Ha and said, almost under his breath, "Does your husband have a drinking problem?"

John, whose auditory perception had always been advanced, said, "Don't worry Mr. Dung. I ordinarily have far more drinks than problems and far fewer problems when I drink. Cheers." He raised his glass and Mr. Dung mimicked him; when the glasses clinked John smiled as if the sound pleased him. "Now to the question of origin," John said.

Mr. Dung looked confused, and Ha said, in Vietnamese, "He's talking about nationality."

"Nationality," Mr. Dung said in his accented English.

"Do you propose that a man who is born in a country does not then belong to the country in which he was born?" John said.

Ha whispered some words in Vietnamese into Mr. Dung's ear.

"You look Japanese," Mr. Dung said.

"And so, the way you look is always in accord with the country you are born to, as it is in Vietnam? Yes, but is that always the case?"

"I don't think he understands, dear," Ha said.

"Is there an infallible relation between one's appearance and the country of one's birth?"

Mr. Dung looked confused and stirred the sliced pork in his rice bowl. "Why you don't like being Japanese?"

"Au contraire," John said. "I *love* the subtle flavor of sushi, the delicate brevity of haiku, the unparalleled courage of the samurai, the evocative quietism of Ozu, the whimsical fancy of Miyazaki."

"I think my husband's a little tired. Off to bed," she said, putting her hand on John's shoulder.

"I suppose I am tired," he said. Then to Mr. Dung: "Don't take a word I say seriously, no more than you would your grandson's babble about Mickey and Pluto. I've enjoyed a few glasses which makes me more direct when discretion is my true nature as you'll see in the morning. Goodnight, Mr. Dung."

Ha sliced, diced, and washed alongside Mr. Dung's wife, a trueborn housewife with the patience of a Siberian tiger. How can Mrs. Dung do it? John thought. Every day the same routine—grocery, shopping, cooking, cleaning; then the rambunctious grandsons for whom the Dung house was a far more affordable daycare centre. Ha too became entrapped in the web of culinary arts, and reading to the boys, ages two and four, like a nanny. John helped with dicing, cleaning, washing the dishes, reading *Beauty and the Beast* and *Aladdin* to the older boy, and genuinely enjoying the art of storytelling. He was pleased to think himself a good houseguest, someone who contributed to the ongoing events of the host family.

At the end of their third day in the Dung house, with no word from the embassy yet about Ha's and John's Canadian work permits, Ha's face appeared drained of colour. Who was this Ha, John thought, scowling at the little boys, her shoulders slumped, a look of quiet desperation in her eyes?

"I think we need to divorce." Ha suddenly announced. She and John had their ups and downs like any couple, but nothing had occurred in their three years together to warrant separation.

"A divorce?" John said. "You have to cook and take care of kids, and so you want a divorce?" John was a full foot taller than Ha, and at forty, he was five years older; this discrepancy sometimes gave him license to analyze.

"This is a separate thing I've been thinking about for a while."

"You haven't had time to think. When did this thinking happen?"

"Mr. Dung made me see something about you," Ha said.

"He opened your eyes, huh?" John said.

"He said you have bad habits like sleeping in and drinking wine and reading too much."

"Let me demonstrate something for you." John walked across the room, his right leg dragging behind his left, just as it had done a month before when he strained his hamstring. "Why do you think this injury hasn't healed?" Ha stayed slumped against the wall, her face lacking affect. "Because I've been working so hard helping you in the kitchen and looking after Mr. Dung's grandchildren, and this I suppose is my reward. Divorce?"

"You work, but I have to work so much more," Ha said. "Mr. Dung demands fresh meals every day, no leftovers, and at least three new dishes per meal, Mrs. Dung told me."

"So, you have divorced me, and taken Mr. Dung as your husband it seems."

"Mr. Dung said you're not good enough for me, you don't have as much energy as other men and you don't guide my son well."

"Mr. Dung said this, Mr. Dung said that. Are you talking about Mr. Dung or Confucius?"

"I don't know what to think. My mind's all twisted up. Let's talk about this again in a few days," Ha said, rubbing her eyes.

In the morning, John walked downstairs in his pyjamas for breakfast. An was reclined on the sofa playing video games. Mr. Dung hovered over the child. "Stop play video games, read books," Mr. Dung said. An didn't bother to respond or even look up. "Stop play, An, stop play."

John filled a mug all the way to the top with dark roast coffee, took a few sips, then poured in a generous amount of cream. "So good," he said. Then he brought the coffee into the living room where Mr. Dung was instructing An on the pleasures of reading books.

"Good morning, Mr. Dung," John said. "It's always so nice to meet a fellow reader. Ha always complained I only read dead white males, so I've moved on to the women and I sure don't regret it. Women, whether it's Emily Bronte or Elizabeth Bowen or Ursula Le Guin, give us a nuance, a picture of how people interact that the Phillip Roth's and Hemingway's of the world don't necessarily give. Don't you think so, Mr. Dung?"

"I couldn't agree more," Mr. Dung said. "Maybe you take An to bookstore later?"

In the afternoon John took An to Perspective Books. They walked through the aisles.

"You know An, in high school they used to call me the Fat Knight. I wasn't fat, but we had to read this play *Henry IV*, which had this funny character Falstaff. Our English teacher Mr. Brightman called Falstaff the Fat Knight. Falstaff was really funny, and I was the class clown, so everyone started calling me The Fat Knight."

"That's actually a pretty cool nickname," An said.

"Could have been worse," John said. "So, if you insist on changing your name to Ansel in Canada, I'm not going to put up a fight. You work it out with your mom."

"She and Mr. Dung think I'd be betraying my culture if I changed my name, but I feel more like an Ansel than an An."

"The only thing I know is," John said, "if you feel like an Ansel, you probably are one. That's just between us, by the way."

 Poor Mrs. Dung, John thought, to have to serve hand and foot all her life and all the days to come until she's too frail to cook and scrub. An dug in, chopsticks firmly in his left hand.

"Eat with right hand!" Mr. Dung said. Mr. Dung must have had enough of this child's petulance, for he related the story about how, in India, people wiped their asses with their left hands and so ate with their right hands. Clearly, it was unhygienic if not downright filthy to eat with your left hand.

"You haven't been anywhere near India; what do you have to do with them?" John said. "I have six Indians working under me, making engines."

"If memory serves me, New Delhi is about 5,000 miles away from Hanoi and we're even further than that from either here in Hoosier-ville," John said.

"Eat with right hand," Mr. Dung said.

"Did you know that Leonardo da Vinci and Keanu Reeves are left-handed, by any chance?" John said.

"I don't care. I care An eats with right hand."

"The poor child cannot manage rice with his off-hand any more than I can shoot jump shots with my left hand," John said.

Ha inserted herself here: "An, eat with your right hand, do as Mr. Dung says."

An made a gallant effort and with some patience brought a few grains of rice to his mouth.

"This pork is lovely," John said, looking at Mrs. Dung.

"Thank you," Mrs. Dung said. "It's a traditional northern Vietnamese dish."

"I killed the pig," Mr. Dung said, laughing.

"I beg your pardon?" John said.

"I kill pig, cut it, Mrs. Dung cook it. I kill pig on your plate." Suddenly Mr. Dung was full of mirth and smiling from ear to ear.

"You haven't killed a pig in your life," John said, giggling. This comment inspired Mr. Dung to rifle through his iPhone until he found a picture of him and his friends in Moscow in their college student days butchering, or at least skinning and taking apart a dead pig, sometime in the 1970s. "Do you want me to kill you?" Mr. Dung said. The statement was so outrageous that John attributed it to a syntactical error common to second-language learners of English. John scanned the table and saw that either Mr. Dung's remark hadn't registered, or the others simply didn't hear what he said. Whatever the case was, John excused himself, blaming a rare but significant case of heartburn, and retreated up the stairs to his bedroom.

An hour later, Ha opened the door to the bedroom. "It was rude of you to walk away suddenly at dinner," she said.

"Pardon?" John said. He expected Ha to be sympathetic.

"It was rude," Ha repeated, glaring now.

"I thought it was a tad impolite to threaten someone's life," John said.

"You're a guest in his house."

"Need you remind me?"

"He doesn't speak English well; you should forgive him."

"I thought he pronounced the word 'kill' quite clearly, didn't you?"

"Maybe he didn't say 'kill.' Maybe he said another word," Ha suggested.

"Like what?" John said. "Shrill, dill, fill?"

"Don't mind what Mr. Dung says. You'd be oozing with

sympathy for me if you knew how many cucumbers I chopped today. And that grandson weeps hysterically if he's not held."

"My heart goes out to you. I'm sorry."

"I'm sorry too, for threatening divorce. You know I couldn't do without you." John and Ha made love for the first time in ten days. An played the role of housemaid and John was lord of the manor, paddle in hand and foul-mouthed the way Ha liked it.

John was woken by the sound of the grandsons yelling and running up and down the stairs. The oldest grandson, Map, poked his head into the bedroom and, upon being perceived by John, let out a scream of glee and bolted back down the stairs. When John came down, he saw Mr. Dung holding Map. Somehow, in the span of time it took for John to walk down a single flight of stairs, Map had lost his mind and was now crying and pelting Mr. Dung's face with his fists. John expected Mr. Dung to come down hard on Map for punching him square in the face multiple times, but he didn't; he coddled the boy. Map, while he had his Vietnamese mother's and grandmother's eyes, had light brown hair and a whitish skin tone that made him look altogether more Irish than Asian. Here and there, he took after his mother; holistically, his father's imprint was more conspicuous.

After the boys were retrieved by their father, John, Mr. Dung, and An sat at the breakfast table. An shook the bottle of maple syrup rather violently because there was only a little bit left at the bottom.

"Don't shake so much," Mr. Dung said. "You have to be more careful in this country."

"Why *this* country?" An said.

"You immigrant here, so you have to learn."

"I'm not an immigrant," An said, his mouth full of waffles.

"Are you an American?" Mr. Dung said, smiling, as if he'd just beaten An at a game of blackjack. In An's heart and mind he was an American. It was only on paper that he wasn't. He knew no other country as home, and he said "God bless America" without a trace of irony.

John took a sip of his coffee and said, "If An isn't American, I don't know who is."

"He from Vietnam," Mr. Dung said, throwing his hands in the air.

"It's not a matter of where you're from, but of who you are, isn't it?" John said.

"You don't get to be, just because you feel you are," Mr. Dung said.

"I don't see why not. How else do we know who we are, but that we feel we are what we are?" John said, waving his arm in the air.

When guests make a prolonged visit to relatives, they are obliged to attend events they would otherwise have declined. This was the case with Mr. Dung's daughter's gender reveal party. Ha felt it was her duty to help Hue prepare for the party. She shopped for pink and blue plastic cups, napkins, and balloons. She even helped bake the cake. Ha stayed out of the planning for the guessing game for guests because it seemed beyond her cultural understanding. Hue was a near-native speaker of English and came to the US at the age of ten. For Hue, it was second nature to marry her white midwestern American husband and to spend holidays with his relatives who drove out from rural towns on the outskirts, towns Hue had barely heard of but its various routes she had now committed to memory. She and her husband Mike would make the occasional drive out to the outposts and Hue found these places quaint and oddly charming, rather than hegemonic and stifling. The women—Hue, Hue's mother, Ha, and Mike's sisters—collectively cooked, cleaned, and decorated the house.

On the day of the gender reveal party—about halfway through the event—Hue made an announcement to the small coterie of guests. She thanked Mike's "marvelous" sisters for coming into town and helping with the prep work to make this effusion of blue and pink possible. The name "Ha" did not escape Hue's lips, though Ha watched closely to see if acknowledgement would come. It didn't, and it wasn't about to; that was clear from the way Hue avoided even looking at Ha.

Mr. Dung kept himself to the edges of the event, refilling the empty rows of water bottles on the folding table, bringing in more ice, more soft drinks, half-mumbling words to himself that no one, even if they stood close and listened carefully, could distinguish as either English or Vietnamese or a mixture of both. Hue did not make an attempt to bring her father into the mix, to thank him in an off-handed way as she would sometimes do at family gatherings when only her Vietnamese side of the tribe was in attendance.

Occasionally Mr. Dung tried to crack a joke but his son-in-law, Mike, and his father, Weldon, a man who looked like he might have just stepped down from a tractor, didn't engage him in conversation. Mike's side of the family was, if rural, open-minded, and accepting, happily welcoming; but none of them went out of the way to pat Mr. Dung on the back and tease him, as they did to Mike's friends. They were not ignoring Mr. Dung. They sat, smiled, and chatted about their hometowns. It was Mr. Dung who did not have the words to say, at least not in their language; he would have been the life of the party in his own language, he thought. Now he was lurking in the corners, opening, and closing things.

John made his way into conversation with Weldon by way of the Indianapolis Colts. Though a fan of the San Francisco 49ers, representing, as they did, his home region allegiance, John knew a few things about the Colts. He offered what he thought about their quarterback situation and Weldon and John got along by sheer dint of exchanging players' names and pronouncements of who's over-the-hill and still-has-it and should-be-traded and should-be given-one-last-chance, the way men of a certain stripe —a dying breed—can suddenly mythologize their perceptions through trivial talk of football teams.

When Mr. Dung saw his son-in-law talking with John, he nudged An over to the corner of the sofa where the conversation was taking place.

"Talk, talk as much as you can," he said. "Talk like an American, with Americans."

An came over and seated himself.

"I overheard only a little of what you guys were talking about," An said. "I'm afraid I know as much about football as I know about molecular biology. Actually, I probably know more about molecular biology."

"You're 12," John said. "You know nothing about any type of biology."

"I bet he does," Weldon said, beaming.

John saw Mr. Dung hugging the wall, and picking up paper towels from the floor. He turned to Weldon and said, "Mr. Dung has been very kind to take us in. He's been worried about An fitting in, fitting into American society."

"He's always been a generous man," Weldon said. "An seems to be doing just fine."

The fledgling camaraderie, vulnerable and sustainable as strips of paper, was interrupted only by the game that would reveal the gender: there was a piñata and guests were slapping at it with a stick. An gave it a few blows but none of them scratched the surface. Then one of Mike's sisters, the oldest one, Mary, took a crack and there was an explosion of blue confetti. There was something anticlimactic about the information embedded in these small blue bits since everyone knew it was a boy. Then John, who had been watching people take futile whacks at the piñata, felt Ha tugging at his sleeve. It was time to go.

The second time Ha proposed divorce, John had just about had it, if he hadn't had it already. "That's it, I'm taking you and An out of here tomorrow," John said.

"Where would we go? We can't afford it," Ha said.

"We'll go to a cheap motel; I'll pay for it." John knew Ha was furious at Hue for not acknowledging her hard work for the gender reveal party. She always felt like Hue looked down on her for being Vietnamese, born and raised. Hue was too but she came to America at ten and was born and raised again in a new way in a new country. Ha on the other hand did not make it to the States until graduate school beckoned, at the ripe age of twenty-nine.

John searched through Priceline and found an end-of-summer sale at the Super 8 in a college town 120 miles up north. They made up a story about why they had to leave; some bogus account about needing to access a university library for Ha's new job. John would break the news to Mr. Dung in the morning.

They spent the morning packing their things and cleaning up around the house as if the achievement of chores would ease the abruptness of their departure. By the time they left, it was early evening.

Mrs. Dung was none too pleased as Ha's sudden, inexplicable departure—puzzling to both Mrs. Dung and surely to Ha's parents in Vietnam as well—might cast a bad light on Mrs. and Mr. Dung, though she could not calculate with any precision what sort of light would be cast. Mrs. Dung only had a vague foreboding of something vaguely irreputable smearing her standing with Ha's family back in Hanoi. John could never have guessed at such intimations, and naively assumed that Mrs. Dung objected merely out of a desire to help this fledgling family out. That was how John's mother would have reacted to the early departure of house guests, and he presumed a universal characteristic from the way his parents ran their home.

"We're sorry for torturing you, Mr. Dung. We'll be out of your hair now," John said.

"No, not torture," Mr. Dung said, putting his hand on John's shoulder.

"Thanks for trying to help An," John said, shaking Mr. Dung's hand.

"Make sure he eats with his right hand," Mr. Dung said.

"I'll do the best I can," John said. "We appreciate it."

When they reached the motel, it was already getting dark out. The motel was situated directly next to a gas station which was set inexplicably next to another gas station, sat to the left of a steakhouse. An intoxicated, bearded man with disheveled blonde hair and no shirt sat on the grass, and two police officers questioned him—about what, John didn't care to find out.

The room, though containing two full-size beds, was smaller than a bachelor's studio. The ceiling looked like craters on the moon. Seeing the dive John had brought the family to, with its view of the interstate, big cargo trucks passing by, and a particular telephone pole made unique somehow for being the only one framed by their small window, he felt guilt-stricken. He was sure Ha would protest, perhaps insist on a return to the Dung residence.

Instead, Ha put her suitcase on the floor, unzipped it with relish, and plucked her pyjamas off the top of the neatly folded pile. Then she threw her arms around John. "I love you, darling," she said. "Let's have babies together." The flush of youth seemed to return to Ha's cheeks, and she looked just as pretty as before they had become guests at the grand house of misfortune.

"Shall we grab a bite to eat?" he said.

"There's a Denny's across the street. I hear they have a stunning Grand Slam," An said.

"I'm famished," Ha said.

They crossed the four-lane expressway in the dark, dodging one pickup truck after another. John put his arm around An's slumped shoulder and pulled his slight form close. "I'll do the best I can," he said to himself. When they got to the other side, they saw the silhouette of rabbits walking across a lawn, briefly illuminated by streetlights, before vanishing over a small hill.

HERITAGE

BY RILEY-GRACE AVELINA HUGGINS

When I made my mother review my college application before I submitted it, she pointed out that I'd forgotten to check off on the application that I'm Asian.

"Am I supposed to?" I asked her.

She looked at me in disbelief. "Yes. Your grandmother was from the Philippines."

Years later, I searched on the internet: *Am I still Asian American if I am white? Is it okay to call myself Asian American if I don't have Asian culture? How do I help my dad heal from the effects of racism? Am I still Asian American if I can't speak Tagalog?* Google has never had answers for me.

I grew up in Texas. Girls in my third-grade class were from Mexico and Puerto Rico. They would ask me, "Are you sure you're not Mexican?"

"No, my grandma is from the Philippines."

"Oh. Have you been to the Philippines?"

"No, she came here in the sixties. And besides, she died before my parents met." All that I knew about my grandmother was filtered through the lens of my grandfather, a quiet, looming man. He would tell stories, recount the war, or drop tidbits of genealogy at each family gathering, all the while sitting in a corner surveying the room, his white hair glistening. Anything he told me about his late wife never satisfied the insatiable appetite I had for information about her. He was tall, she was short. He was white, she was not. He was in the Navy, she lived in Bacoor.

My dad is half-Filipino, while my mom is proudly Irish with green eyes and fair hair. She learned to cook adobo and tilapia and lumpia when she married my dad. It was a love letter to him, to us. Something to honour the woman she and I both admired and had never met.

The older I got, the more I started to look like my mom. My broad nose changed shape to slim and delicate, and in the summer, sprayed with freckles. I haven't been able to tan like my dad, dark in the summer, since elementary school.

In middle school, my mom would occasionally cook only vegan meals for a month. We would take family trips to Central Market to peruse the exotic fruit section. For me, going to Central Market meant buying boxes of Botan rice candy to eat on the trip home. My dad had introduced the candy to my brother and me. He had told us that my grandmother had eaten them during her childhood, and he had eaten them during his, too. Eating them was a ritual I always looked forward to. I still buy them now whenever I find them. I can't leave tiny candy stores or Asian markets until I do.

During a family vacation the summer before I started high school, my father lost consciousness twice, at Grand Central Station and at a Mexican restaurant in Texarkana. Both times, his face had suddenly turned deathly purple, his eyes glazed over, and he fell onto the ground. We admitted him to have emergency heart surgery. Because my siblings and I were too many and too young to visit the recovery ward, our mother called from the hospital to tell us that our dad was okay. She told us that while he was recovering from anesthesia, he had asked the nurse if she wanted to hear all of the swear words he could remember in Tagalog.

My dad often traveled for work when I was young. He was a physician recruiter for twenty years, and he took flights all the time to place doctors in hospitals across the country. Each time he went somewhere new, he would bring back a postcard for me. His flights usually came in at night after I had gone to sleep, so he would give his souvenir to me the next morning before school. I kept them in a stack on my nightstand, photos of Mount Rushmore, Lake Superior, and my favourite, the Mall of America.

Once, when I was eight years old, he arrived home earlier than usual. Eagerly, I asked for my souvenir from Milwaukee.

"Go bring me my carry-on and I'll get it for you," he told me. "I put it right on top of my clothes."

Within moments, I wheeled in his black bag. With hands clasped in anticipation, I looked on as he unzipped his bag and revealed a neon orange slip of paper.

"I get these all the time," he nonchalantly assured my mother who was looking on from the next room. "My bags always get randomly searched."

She raised her brows and said, "It's not random if it happens every time." She told him morosely that the colour of his warm, brown skin should not be cause for concern.

One of my friends from high school, Audrey, had a Filipino mother. She would tell her about me, and her mother would make extra lumpia for Audrey to bring to me. I would save half of them to bring home for my sisters.

When I told Audrey stories about my life and what I knew about my heritage, some imposter syndrome in the back of my mind convinced me that I wasn't "Asian enough." On most days, I mourned the fact that my heritage felt so distant. I didn't know a single word in my grandma's native language, the same language Audrey wove in and out of when she parroted back conversations between herself and her mother.

"You're always welcome to come over. My mom will cook for you," Audrey told me once as we studied for our statistics exam. She would tell me about her grandparents, Lolo and Lola, coming into town. *Lolo and Lola.* I repeated the words over and over again in my head.

I recall some Saturday afternoon when I was fourteen sitting in my grandfather's truck after a lunch visit to his place.

"What was she like?" I asked.

He was silent for so long that I had to turn back to look at him to see if he had even heard me. To my surprise, he was crying.

"She was...amazing. She was so bright. I don't know how to tell you."

I nodded. "Everyone tells me I'm like her but what does that mean?"

"You are like her in every way," he agreed.

My grandpa was seventy-two at this time, and that was the only time I had ever seen him cry. My question remained unanswered.

———

My parents had finalized their divorce in August of my senior year of high school. By that November, my grandfather reached his final days. The first time my grandfather had battled his cancer was something I'd only heard stories about—surgeries and treatments from well before I was born, scars that blended in with tattoos from his days in the Navy. I thought that sickness was like a far-off dream. This time, it was much worse. He was older and weaker. My uncle was the first to break the news to me. He promised me that this time, my grandfather wouldn't win the battle.

My mother handed me her cell phone and a black velvet pouch that I had seen stored in her jewelry box growing up. In the past, whenever I had asked what was in it, she'd tell me that I'd find out when I was older. My grandfather was on the other line of the phone. I didn't know it then but it was the last conversation we would have.

"Hello?" I said into the speaker.

"Gracie." He sounded terrible. "Did your mother give you my gift?" I opened the pouch. Opalescent pearls glimmered back at me. "They were Evelyn's," he said. "I gave them to her as an engagement gift when I was stationed over there in Subic Bay. When your dad got married, they became your mom's. Evelyn wanted you to have them."

"She did?" I asked him. I held the pearls in my hand. It was a set: necklace, bracelet, and earrings. I didn't understand how someone who had never met me could want to give me their engagement gift.

"She wanted them to go to her first granddaughter." His voice was quiet and a million miles away.

I thanked him for the gift and wished him a good night. He told me he loved me and hung up the phone.

After the phone call, my mother and I laid on her bed and examined the pearls. "When did she wear them, do you know?" I asked. I held the set in my hands, tilting them this way and that so that they glinted in the lamplight. I wanted to imagine them around my grandmother's neck but I had no visual memory of her.

"To dinners and special events, I think," Mom answered as she took the bracelet from my palm and held it up to her own wrist. "I wore them to my rehearsal wedding dinner."

I watched from the outside as a memory played in her head.

She smiled and handed it back to me. "You could wear them when you graduate in the spring."

My grandfather died on the first day of December, and his funeral came quickly afterwards. I wore a black dress I bought on sale from Old Navy and in my anxiousness chewed the inside of my mouth so hard I had a fat lip for days. I didn't go up to the casket. I watched as my father kissed his father on the forehead.

My aunt gave the eulogy. She told a story I'd never heard before, one of my grandfather being punished for going back to see my grandmother when he was restationed.

"He never stopped going back for her," my aunt said. "He went back to her then and brought her to America with him."

There was so much about their love that I would never know and will never get to ask. The answers are lost somewhere below their shared burial plot.

———

In the winter of my sophomore year of college, my father moved three hours away. In the months before that, I dropped in for the occasional dinner, went on family vacations with him, and did my best to answer his phone calls. We had attempted to be cordial since the funeral, but it would never be like it was when I was a kid. The move had made it even harder.

I went to visit him with my siblings and helped him decorate his new house for Christmas. We talked about how different things had been since the divorce, now that he and mom didn't share the holidays. I hadn't spent a Christmas with him since the first winter after the divorce. We talked about what winter festivities would be like when I had a family of my own.

"What will your children call me?" he asked.

"Lolo, I imagine."

"Lolo! That's right!" He remarked that he had called his own grandfather that, a lifetime ago.

I smiled. "Do you think if your mom was alive, we would call her Lola?"

He pondered this. I imagined her here, all four feet, zero inches of her standing next to me. Even my youngest sibling, my seven-year-old brother, would have been taller than her. "I've never thought about it, but I suppose you would."

In May of that year, I sat at a beach with my mom, processing my thoughts. I told her, "I want to say I'm Asian American, I want to say I'm mixed race, I want to claim all these identities, but I know I haven't felt the same pain that so many other Asian Americans have. I haven't grown up with the same culture, you know? I mean, I eat the foods, I have the hair, yet I don't have their skin nor eyes, or language. It doesn't feel like *my* heritage. It's not my right, I haven't earned that privilege."

She was silent for a long time. Then, in the same quiet voice she'd used when I cried as a child, she told me, "Your grandma Avelina was the strongest woman I've ever known, and I only know her through stories. She left her whole life behind for your grandfather, for a whole new world she didn't know. She went from her family and friends in the Philippines to middle-of-nowhere East Texas, and they were not kind to her, your dad, nor your uncle. They called them names. They excluded them. But she was powerful and could not be stopped or hindered. It wasn't until they took her heart out of her body on an operating table that she stopped. You have her hair, her name, but most importantly, you have that same strong, powerful, and unstoppable heart. *That* is your heritage."

Reading Materials for the Afterlife

by Katia Lo Innes

It was always easier to cut through the old landfill. The dump, which had been rechristened Euston Park, was converted into public green space half a century ago. Beth tried to imagine what garbage lay beneath its grassy slopes. She pictured broken IBM punch cards, telephone wires—technology from her mother's near-ancient youth. Now, beautiful allergens like Queen Anne's Lace and ragweed sprouted in Euston Park.

It was easier to cut through on a bike, even during a hot summer day. The Southwestern sun and humidity radiating from the nearby Great Lakes made this type of mid-July day pleasurably uncomfortable, the heat swaddling you head-to-toe like a weighted blanket. Cutting through Euston Park avoided Wharncliffe Road's traffic, and for a young cyclist such as Beth, offered a covert path to reach the Dairy Queen and Taco Bell.

That was how—even during a government-issued heat and humidity warning—Beth found herself standing on the pedals of her Canadian Tire mountain bike, hoisting her way uphill through the park. Her younger brother Peter lagged behind her, and she could hear his strained breaths as they powered up the steep incline. They were hungry; nothing had been prepared for supper that night, and the President's Choice chocolate granola bars in the cupboards had done nothing to satiate the gnawing in their stomachs. Occasionally, Beth would turn back to check if Peter was in her line of vision: if he wasn't, she would stop and wait for him to catch up, a tiny brown speck on wheels. Under the sun Beth and Peter became two shades darker than the rest of their neighbours. Beth cherished this time, secretly pleased that her dark hair lightened to reveal honey brown streaks.

Reaching the top of the hill, Beth let her feet touch the ground so that she could better survey her ascent. The sun hung low, grazing the treetops. Peter heaved his way beside her, sweat suctioning his thin t-shirt onto his back.

"Which is," Peter asked, inhaling the soupy air in large gulps. "The way to the Dairy Queen?"

Beth paused for a moment and inspected the scene before her. The path forked into three smaller paths, one of which veered sharply into a forested lot. That definitely wasn't it, she reasoned, so it must be the one farthest to the right that curved around the wooded area. Beth could spot the electrical posts behind it.

"It's the one to the right," she pointed.

Peter frowned. "Are you sure?"

Beth nodded. "I'm positive."

She pushed forward on her bike, letting gravity's momentum pull her downhill. Peter followed closely behind, their juvenile skeletons rattling over each bump. The path looped aimlessly through the tall grass; electric wires dangled overhead, intermittently strewn with tied-up pairs of shoes. Beth put one pedal in front of the other, inching her way closer to the main road. She counted the number of bends in the path—one, two, three. Strange, she remembered only having to turn twice.

"Beth," Peter called from behind. "I don't know where we are."

Resigned, Beth's feet fell to the ground. They had ended up near a stack of concrete barriers littered with black garbage bags. Euston Park's former career as a dumping ground continued into its new life. Beth ignored Peter's pleas and edged closer to the junk, her eye caught by the technicolour sheen of a magazine stack piercing through a blue recycling bag.

Beth abandoned her bike and thumbed through the magazines. *People's, US Weekly,* the usual tabloid suspects. No *Vogue* nor *Vanity Fair,* nothing too high calibre. She kept flipping through and froze, landing on a *Maxim* issue. Not one, but a dozen *Maxim* issues spooning each other, sticky in the humid air. Beth had always seen these magazines behind the corner store register, eyes peering at her through the frosted plastic cover slips. Beth—who could not bear to look at a cashier directly—marvelled at the directness of these women as they stared back at her from their glossy spreads. Cautiously, she picked one up—

"Dead bird!" Peter yelled. "Beth, over here."

Beth hastily put the magazines down, brushed her hands on her jean shorts, and went to go stand beside Peter. At his feet lay a dead robin, its wings askew and head splayed to the side.

"Oh eeerck," gagged Beth.

"Looks like a dog got to it." Peter said. "Or a cat even. Or a coyote—did you know coyotes live in London?"

"No way a coyote did this," Beth argued. "Come on, let's go."

"Wait," Peter insisted. "We should bury it. Like *tai po.*"

Beth weighed her options. Visions of roadkill past flashed in her mind: animals flattened across country backroads with their organs spilling out, left in the sun. The pancaked raccoon at the foot of their driveway last fall, which caused Beth to burst into tears on her walk to school. Peter nudged it with his toe, expecting the corpse to have some give. Instead, the bird was stiff, arthritic. Jerky-like. Beth swallowed and fixed her gaze on the bird's blank visage.

She considered turning around, getting back on her bike and leaving the bird to rot, alone. She imagined what would happen if larger mammals found it, and all the ways it would deteriorate; how its tiny white bones would protrude, feathers matted until it became unrecognizable. And the summer heat would only amplify the rotting stench of addled flesh melding with melting plastic and gasoline. A gaping hole had emerged between her and the bird: the living and the dead. The corpse taunted her— while she struggled to figure out where she would get her dinner, the bird held no anxieties towards its future. It was fixed. Unwavering, It held more certainty in its three-inch frame than Beth did in her entire body. Beth needed to act on this, and act fast.

"Okay fine," she decided. "We'll bury him."

"Where?" Peter asked.

"Here," Beth replied, using the heel of her shoe to scuff at the ground. She was on her hands and knees now, digging wildly with her fingers, trying to breach dirt in vain. Peter got on his knees to help but she pushed him aside.

"Let me do it," she insisted.

The skin on her knuckles split against the gravel but she continued to dig stubbornly, blood peeling out from under her fingernails.

"Beth, stop," Peter urged. She was making little progress. "You're hurting yourself."

Beth leaned back on her heels, her breath ragged and dog-like. Blood oozed from the lacerations on her fingers.

"We can put it here instead," Peter suggested, gesturing to a small opening beneath the concrete barriers.

"Yeah, it can be like a, uh, what's it called?" Beth stammered.

"Mausoleum," Peter stated.

Beth turned to him. "You're getting smart," she laughed. Peter smiled.

They entombed the bird in a shoebox coffin, wedged underneath the concrete slab. For flair, they shoved in a roll of *US Weekly*—reading materials for the afterlife, they rationalized. With her house keys, Beth scratched a shoddy crucifix above the entrance and an estimated epitaph (b. 2009-2011). Of course they knew the cross would be the first to go, swept away with wind and rain. The magazines would decompose and dissolve into dirt. Even so, they marked the bird as best as they could. The two children stood at the foot of the tomb.

"What should we do now?" Peter asked.

Beth thought for a moment. "We should pray."

"I don't know how to pray," Peter replied glumly.

"Do you just want to go to Dairy Queen instead?"

They both looked at Beth's hands and burst out laughing.

"Another time," she replied. "We have frozen pizza at home."

Beth turned to pick up her bike, streaking blood on the handles. Her pulse thumped dully in her hands. She packed the rest of the magazines in her bag and slung it over her shoulder.

Peter didn't bother with any goods; instead, he grabbed a fistful of Queen Anne's lace and stuffed it into his back pocket. They peddled back in the dark, tire chains clicking peacefully under yellowed street lamps. It took all of five minutes for Beth to begin feeling lightheaded, black spots bursting like overripe cherry tomatoes pressed into her eye sockets. The heaviness of the night had caught up with her no matter how fast she pedalled. Her feet fell against the ground and she slung her forearms onto her handles.

"The bus," she managed between breaths, "Let's take the bus. I'm too tired."

They stashed their bikes behind a dumpster, concealed deftly behind broken-down cardboard boxes. The night bus took its time. They had nowhere to go and nothing else to do, so they waited. Thirty minutes passed. The blood on Beth's hands had crusted over and she examined them, letting the scabs crack as she stretched her fingers, feeling the new layers of skin grow taut. The bus still did not come and she grew increasingly irritated; if she could divine trash into treasure, if she could lead a bird into the afterlife, surely she could will a bus to run on time.

A seagull had perched itself on the bus sign. *Parking lot gulls would be a better name*, Beth's father once joked. The bird was far from the shore but maybe it still believed it was at the sea, maybe it wished to be at the beach but had given up on its way, landing on this street as a compromise.

Sheepishly, the bus pulled up to the stop. Beth and Peter climbed on.

"We don't have any—" she began, but it didn't matter. The bus driver shrugged and got off the bus to have a smoke, ushering the children on.

Peter took a seat near the back as Beth watched the driver bring the lighter to his mouth. Watching the thin gauze of smoke trail from the cigarette, she was reminded of how her friend Sarah's house reeked of cigarettes, and how the smell lingered on Sarah's father when he walked past her. How she ached to get closer to him, just to inhale him deeper. She would remember this scent many years later; her eyes heavy with beer and desire, anonymous hands pulling her onto the bed.

Back at the bus stop another gull had landed on the bench, cooing demurely beside its companion. Then, another landed. And another. As if there were a secret signal emanating from the bus stop. Seemingly every bird in the city of London had descended on the vehicle, not just gulls, but robins, too. Birds clambered onto the bench and fluttered up to the bus, enveloping it in motion. They swarmed relentlessly, picking at the flaking paint, picking at each other. Beth could hear the din of complaint rising from the other passengers, but she didn't mind.

"Beth, are you seeing this?" gaped Peter.

Beth watched in awe. Maybe the birds will latch onto the bus and pick it up, she hoped, carrying it far far away to somewhere where the words "lake effect" have no meaning. The throng was so dense now that it completely obscured the windows, rendering the inside of the bus dark—an avian solar eclipse. The bus rattled and shook, preparing for airborne transit. The sounds grew louder and louder into a cacophony of birdsong. Beth and Peter's own late night chorus. Sensing the miraculous, the birds began to leave one by one until all was quiet. The driver, who had stood in awe as the flock descended, yanked the door open, and threw himself into his chair with a huff, mechanically shifting gears and revving the bus into motion.

Beth and Peter looked at each other, sharing a smile. No one bothered to look at them, or even stop to inquire about the dried blood covering Beth's hands and jeans. It didn't matter, because they had heard the birdsong when no one else could. The bus sleepwalked through the residential streets, dropping the children off on their block.

The lights were off in the dining room; if they had been on, they would have illuminated the fine layer of dust that had begun to accumulate on the wood table. Beth stuck her hands under the faucet and winced as the cold water flushed out the dirt and grass crusted into her skin. The red water ran clear against the porcelain after a minute. Once they'd finished sharing pepperoni pizza, Beth made sure Peter brushed his teeth, taking care not to disturb his dark curls as she pulled his pyjama shirt over his head.

"I think you're a good sister," Peter said to Beth, looking at her in the mirrored medicine cabinet.

"Thank you," Beth replied.

It was the only appropriate response; she felt too young to receive such a compliment. Hot, fat tears burst out of her eyes, and she cried for the bird, and for herself, but she did not understand this yet. Peter hugged her waist, and she let her arms wrap around him. She would've wrapped her arms around the whole world if she could.

The house was as silent as a prayer. Beth turned off all the lights and put Peter to bed before heading to her room. She looked towards the head of her bed frame, wishing someone were kind enough to mark it with a cross.

THE VIGIL

BY MARCEL GOH

I realize now, looking back, just how unusual it had been for my family to have entrusted three children with the overnight watch of a corpse.

It was the third night of the wake, held on the open-air void deck beneath the Jurong housing block where Ah Gong had lived and where Ah Ma would continue to live by herself. Six round tables, each covered with a white plastic sheet and accompanied by flimsy red chairs, were arranged around the slabs of bleached concrete that supported fifteen more storeys of concrete above us. During the day, people who had known our grandfather sat at these tables to play mahjong and eat shelled peanuts. Off to the side was a rectangular table with gas burners on it. Every evening, a catering man simmered vats of soup and curry on them.

At the opposite end of the void deck stood a white tent that housed Ah Gong's shiny wooden coffin. In front of it was a portrait, tinted reddish like many colour photos of that time, from when he'd been young and skinny. People went into this tent to stare and gasp and weep and nod and declare how peaceful Ah Gong looked. These visiting people bored us children, always saying they knew us when we were *this* small, and we had to be good to our Ah Ma now that our Ah Gong was gone. To escape this, we spent much of the daytime upstairs sleeping, and so we didn't get over our jet lag.

Things were different at night, however. The deserted, fluorescently lit void deck became electric with menacing possibility. The two previous nights we'd performed this vigil with our parents, but we had proven ourselves trustworthy and they didn't find the job quite as glamorous as we did, so now it was just us—stalwart defenders of order and tranquility, aged ten, nine, and six.

Being the eldest, I was technically the boss, but my sister was a militaristic, commanding child, which made me mostly a figurehead. This was in the days before she fully accepted a female identity, when she wore her hair short and insisted on being called Jo. Little Roland was our lackey—at that age he was still loyal, stupid, and affectionate, more of a cute durian-headed pet or work beast to us than an actual person.

To pass the time we made up games and feasted on the endless supply of snacks. One was called Taste Your Testbuds. It had originally been called Test Your Tastebuds but Roland had said it wrong once and the name stuck. You closed your eyes and someone fed you a fruit Mento and you had to say what colour it was. We stopped playing when our tongues stung from the acid and we got too good, even Roland guessed correctly more than half the time.

In our next game, the goal was to get a ball of rolled-up Ferrero Rocher foil into an overturned cup in the fewest hits possible. It was aptly named Golf. As clubs, we used the bendy straws from boxes of Vitasoy and Yeo's Lemon Barley Drink. I went first, and at each hole my score was considered par against which my siblings' points were calculated. On the scoresheet, we all sported the surname Woods. The courses became more and more inventive as the night went on. In one, we went into the stairwell and chipped the ball down two flights of stairs; in another, we teed off from the top of Ah Gong's coffin.

This game kept us entertained well past three o'clock. We'd been told that one of the adults would be down around six.

Our father was Ah Gong's firstborn, so the funeral's logistical burdens fell to him, and he and my mother had quickly overcome their jet lag from sheer exhaustion. This was the first time we got some inkling of what had made him and my mother leave Singapore. It wasn't the search for economic opportunity, as with previous generations. Like many in the modern wave, they'd both had stable corporate jobs when they moved five years before. They threw their careers away to live in the wastelands of Canada, where my father was unemployed for a whole year. A reckless thing to do at the best of times but unspeakably irresponsible when you had young mouths to feed. At least, was what our grandfather thought. To my father, the austerity was worth it in return for emancipation from rigid Singaporean society, and it was clear, watching him organize Ah Gong's funeral, that he never possessed the filial piety demanded of a Straits Chinese son.

We'd left the very night we learned of Ah Gong's stroke, and had arrived in time to see him alive but unconscious in the hospital. Our uncle hadn't been so fortunate. He had also left Singapore as soon as he could. At that time he was working in Japan and had only been able to take off work a day after the stroke. Ah Gong had died in the hospital unattended, while our parents were fetching him from the airport. My father's aunts, whose proper names to us were Big Gu Por, 2 Gu Por, and 3 Gu Por, were convinced that the hospital had unplugged Ah Gong while our parents were away.

Even if that were true, so what? was my father's defence. He would have been a vegetable the rest of his life. Anyone should be glad to die in such a merciful way. In the Gu Pors' eyes this was an unforgivable thing to express. The Gu Pors terrified us—with their fierce scowls and incisive cackles, they were like three malevolent witches, always appearing together, conducting loud séances in unintelligible Hokkien, and ratting us out to our parents and grandparents. They were eternally judgemental of the generation below them, and their proclamations were treated as gospel by all the extended family except our father. Because we so feared the Gu Pors we always saw him in a heroic light for standing up to them, but with age we came to realize that many of the skirmishes were a result of unbridled insolence on his part. One episode was because he'd omitted the Gu Pors' names from the newspaper obituary; another had been triggered by his saying he hoped all three of them died together in a freak accident, because he couldn't afford to keep flying home for funerals.

As far as we knew, he didn't cry over Ah Gong's death, but our mother certainly did. She'd lived with my father's family in the months around when I was born, while she and my father saved up for their own place, and she told us how great a man Ah Gong had been. Ah Gong had grown up poor, and had had terrible luck in business, so he worked in his last years as a taxi driver. He got up at five every morning and never left for work before boiling eggs and making kaya toast for everyone, setting each individual place at the table and covering it all with a plastic dome to keep the flies at bay. It was the little things, my mother said, that were most telling of a man's character.

Was this all it took to be considered a great man: providing for one's relatives, adhering to a routine? More or less, according to the ancient creed that governed our family. I suppose that Ah Gong was at least noble in the sense of an inert gas: predictable, steadfast, incorruptible. In a colonial twist, these Confucian traits were seen as symptoms of Ah Gong's unwavering duty to God—the Christian one, that is. A friend had converted him as a young man, and he gradually converted his siblings and cousins. Even his mother, who for many years had held firm against Christianization, pledged herself to Jesus on her deathbed. So in the Gu Pors' eyes, Ah Gong had saved our whole clan from hellfire, and this fact made it all the more outrageous that his own son, my father, had lost touch with God, married a heathen, and was now making a fiasco of his father's memorial ceremonies.

I can only imagine the Gu Pors' reaction if they knew that we unwashed children were the sole protectors of their baby brother's dead body that night. By four o'clock a strong breeze had picked up, which made our foil ball zip around uncontrollably. We'd grown tired of Golf anyway and decided to take our job as guards more seriously. Roland and I filled our pockets with snacks and dragged chairs into Ah Gong's tent to get out of the wind. Jocelyn went into the shrubbery by a nearby playground and returned with small fallen tree branches.

"Why do we need sticks?" asked Roland.

"To protect Ah Gong," I said.

"From what?"

"Dunno, animals. Stray cats."

Jocelyn stood at the opening of the tent and kept watch. "Cats eat people, you know," she said matter-of-factly. "They're too small to attack us alive but they wait for us to die so they can eat our eyeballs. Can you imagine that, Rolo? A cat munching Ah Gong's eyeballs."

Roland was getting spooked. Another favourite game of Jocelyn's and mine was making Roland cry. We had well-defined roles: I was bigger so if it became necessary I dealt physical punishment; meanwhile Jocelyn was something of a verbal enforcer, an expert at emotional manipulation. If we made him cry in the next hour and then spent the hour after that cheering him up, that would keep all of us entertained until six o'clock.

"And you know why they have the wake for five whole days?" continued my sister. "It's to make sure Ah Gong doesn't get *buried alive*." Her eyes widened with manic vigour to emphasize this point to Roland. "So we might need the sticks for that also. If Ah Gong wakes up, Rolo, you run upstairs to get Mummy and Daddy. Me and Oliver will keep him in his box."

Roland nodded. Then he asked, "Can I see Ah Gong again?" and stood on his chair. We slid the panel to peer through the glass at our grandfather's face. He'd died overweight, but he didn't look so fat in death. He wasn't skinny like in the portrait at his feet, but he had lost some pudge nonetheless.

"His eyeballs haven't been ripped out," said Jocelyn and walked back to her post.

Roland and I sat back down. "I'm scared," he said.

"Scared of what?" I snapped.

"Ah Gong waking up."

"If Ah Gong wakes up it's a good thing. It means he's alive."

"Scary though."

"You shouldn't be scared of Ah Gong waking up," said Jocelyn. "You should be scared of animals coming to eat Ah Gong. Or hungry ghosts."

"Ghosts? I don't want to hear about ghosts!" Roland covered his ears.

"No, we have to be ready," she said. "Mummy says there are ghosts everywhere in Singapore."

Unlike my father, my mother was raised under the deeply superstitious Singaporean brand of Buddhism. She never so much as cut across a lawn in Singapore without muttering an apology to any ghost she might have trampled. At night, she said, ghosts were more daring, and you were liable to see or hear them anywhere, not just on unpaved territory. When we asked her if she'd personally seen any, she said no, but that was only because she was a Tiger. Ghosts were afraid of Tigers but the rest of us had to be vigilant. She also believed in reincarnation and other mystical things, so any unnatural goings-on could be messages from our dead ancestors.

A flash of light illuminated the void deck, followed by a deafening peal of thunder. Roland jerked upright and clutched his stick until his knuckles turned white. He clambered onto his chair to make sure the thunder hadn't woken Ah Gong, then walked over to join Jocelyn at the entrance of the tent and scanned the surroundings. It began to rain.

For Roland's benefit Jocelyn recited a lecture she'd gotten from our mother: "If you hear a noise behind you at night, don't just turn your head. They want to trick you, eat your third eye." She placed her index finger on the centre of his forehead and he crossed his eyes to look up at it. "But they can't do it if you turn your whole body around. Your shoulders are like your headlamps. It scares them away. Understand?"

He swallowed and nodded.

Satisfied, she turned back to look outside the tent and gave a shriek, startling both me and my brother. Roland yelled and swivelled his head around wildly, and I jumped to my feet.

"You okay? What is it?" I asked.

"Sorry, sorry," said Jocelyn. "It was just a rat."

"Oh," I said, relieved. "Still, if he comes into the tent, we have to get him."

We paced around, newly aware of the fragility of our grandfather's safety. The rain was coming down loud outside.

A moth flapped into the tent and circled a few times around the lightbulb. It was the biggest moth I'd ever seen, light reddish-grey with black splotches on its wings. We stared at it, mesmerized. It spiralled downwards and landed on the corner of the coffin.

Roland leapt into action. He bashed his stick against the coffin with fervid brutality, missing the moth several times before finally landing a hit. The moth fell to the ground writhing and my brother struck it until it was still. We squatted around the mangled corpse of the moth. What an obese moth.

"Wait, Jo, what if—" I said.

She'd had the same idea. "What if this was Ah Gong reincarnated?" she said.

"What's that mean?" asked Roland.

"Reincarnation is when you die and in your next life you become an animal."

Roland was horrified. He started to wail.

"Ah Gong came to visit us and you killed him, Rolo, how can you be so bad!" said Jocelyn.

"I didn't mean to! I didn't know!" Roland dropped his stick and looked at us for some kind of forgiveness. He sobbed, tears and snot running down his face.

We let Roland cry for a while then felt bad. A part of me really did believe that Ah Gong could come back as a moth. I sat and pondered the violent misunderstanding that had occurred. My sister went into consolation mode. She hugged Roland tight and shushed him over and over and said it was okay.

"Ah Gong is a Christian," I said. "He doesn't believe in reincarnation, so maybe the moth wasn't him."

Once my brother calmed down, we surveyed the damage to the coffin. There were gashes in the wood where he had hit it. We would think of some excuse later. We decided that whether or not it was Ah Gong incarnate, the moth deserved a funeral.

Jocelyn wanted it to be a Viking funeral. She cut a corner off a plastic tablecloth, placed it over our Golf scoresheet, and folded them together into a paper boat that was waterproof on one side. We secured loose ends with some tape we found, then tore strips of newspaper and stuffed them into the boat. Still breathing erratically, Roland picked up the moth and placed it on the pile and for extra fuel, we broke some wood chips off the murder weapon, stacked even more ruffled paper on top of the moth, and added some Mentos wrappers to boot.

We grabbed a lighter from beside the gas burners and walked out towards the open gutter that ran along the side of the housing block. We draped plastic sheeting over the boat to keep it dry. The gutter was a foot wide and about eighteen inches deep. A decent river had formed at the bottom. Big monsoon rain poured down and we were getting soaked. No doubt we'd get a scolding later.

I set the boat down beside the gutter. Roland diligently held the plastic sheet over her hands while Jocelyn clicked the lighter a few times. Nothing happened.

"You have to hold that switch down while you squeeze the trigger," I said.

"Okay, I got it," she said. "I figured it out." A little flame emerged from the end of the barrel. She pressed it into the tangle of paper and the flame growled into life, hissing whenever it met a raindrop on the boat's hull. She and I lowered it into the gutter, where miraculously it stayed upright. The mass of glowing orange floated down the stream of rainwater.

The three of us stood silent. I don't know what my siblings thought of but I thought of Ah Gong. With juvenile agnosticism I imagined him up there with Jesus or in that formless limbo between incarnations. I wondered if he could see us from wherever he was. We'd left Singapore so early in life that I never really got to know him. In my memory he was jolly, his laughter loud and booming, and I wasn't allowed to sit on his armchair by the television unless he was also sitting in it. I was on his lap and he was telling me in his choppy English, "Don't forget, Oliver, you are Hokkien boy. Like your father, like me." But I don't actually remember his deep voice or his thunderous laughter, only *that* they were that way, and now and then when I contemplate what Ah Gong could have meant by telling me I was a Hokkien boy, I think of the impact he had had on all his relatives except his own sons, of his failure to pass down his ideal of how one should care for and honour one's own.

We stood in the rain and blinked water from our eyes, watching the moth's funeral longship get smaller until it rounded a corner, into a culvert under the main road and out of sight.

Famine

by Wayne Mok

Not long after we found out that we couldn't have children, we found the flat. We were visiting our friends' place one night, and on our way out, a young couple entered the lift on the second floor. It looked like they'd just walked out of the latest fall catalogue in neatly hemmed trousers, oxfords, wool coats and cashmere scarves. The girl laughed as she held onto the guy's arm and spoke softly in English with a faint British accent. We caught a glimpse of their front door—an olive-wood door with matte black hardware—as the lift door closed. Standing on opposite sides of the lift, my husband and I glanced at the young couple, and then at each other. I had on a pair of old cargo pants, a floral blouse, and a pilling wool sweater. My husband wore a bright blue windbreaker too big for him over a polo shirt, a pair of baggy jeans, and a pair of running shoes he used for hiking. The couple exited the lift, almost oblivious to our presence. We walked out of the building into the faint glow illuminating the night sky as a thin haze draped itself over Hong Kong Island. My husband pulled out a crumpled tissue from his pocket and sneezed into it.

A few weeks later, we were having morning dim sum at our local teahouse when our friends called. The young couple in the lift were artists—the guy a photographer and director, the girl a producer—they'd just moved to Eastern Europe to work on a long-term conservation project and put their flat on the market, furniture included.

We were first greeted by a foreign scent when we opened the door. It might've been the handcrafted teak furniture or the scented candles—we sniffed and were instantly allured. We stepped inside. It had the same floor plan as our friends' flat, but it felt as if we were in someplace exotic—Bali, Tahiti. Long planks of white oak lined the floors. A set of full-glass bi-fold doors opened up to the large balcony with patio chairs, a grill, and a few baskets of begonias and petunias hanging from the ceiling. Instead of a harbour view, the couple's flat faced south, overlooking a lush collection of tropical shrubbery and trees. There were even a few papaya trees scattered amidst the woods —we imagined seeing a few monkeys hanging from the branches. A set of teak mid-century sofas with leather-covered cushions accompanied a glass coffee table topped with a few of the husband's photography books. There was no television. Instead, there were a pair of bookshelf speakers, a vacuum tube amplifier, a turntable, and a collection of records neatly arranged on a long hi-fi cabinet. The pale-yellow walls inside warmed us up.

The living room opened to the kitchen. Three lamps with shades hung from the ceiling. A matte-black refrigerator rested next to a set of matching ovens. No microwave. A wine fridge was tucked away underneath next to the dishwasher. Large cabinets spanned two walls with a marble-topped island in the centre of the kitchen. An induction stove was encased on one side, while two bar stools accompanied on the other, facing a large single-pane window looking out to the greenery. I had always wanted to cook more.

There was a king-sized bed with white sheets and a fluffy duvet in the middle of the bedroom. A pair of windows to the side opened to more shrubbery. The second room was an office with a standalone glass desk and bookshelves that lined an entire wall, reaching the ceiling. My husband grinned like a five-year-old kid in a candy shop. He was an accountant. The bathroom was too spacious. An antique bathtub with clawed feet sat on the side. Matte black steel fixtures accented the porcelain appropriately. The cold marble floor tickled our feet.

We went home enticed.

We thought of how we would live. We'd host Sunday brunches and dinner parties—cooking would be heaven. We'd have wine and cheese nights—how could we not? On weeknights we'd sprawl out on the sofas, read Ezra Pound to each other, listening to John Coltrane on the phonograph. *Don't worry*, the real estate agent said, *I am sure we can work something out if you are interested*. Yes, we were interested.

We sat down together and gathered our savings, investment, and retirement fund statements and went through them one by one. We visited our banks to see how much we could borrow. We called around to see how much we'd get for our car, our electronics, our furniture, our jewelry, and our current flat. The real estate agent called back a week later. Doable, we said. *We'll be in touch*, she said.

We first let our parents know. *You're moving where?* They asked. It's not too far—there's a bus. *A bus? You're selling your car too?* They sighed. It was a once in a lifetime opportunity. They would understand later. We listed our car, furniture, and electronics in the classifieds. We sold off all our jewelry, except our wedding rings. We put our mid-levels flat on the market. We sold off our investments and applied for a larger mortgage.

We went through our stuff. Catalogues—we threw out a stack we saved from IKEA. Books — we threw out Dan Brown and kept James Joyce. CDs—we threw out the Backstreet Boys and kept Miles Davis. Souvenirs, ornaments, photos—we stuffed them all into cardboard boxes and sealed them, only for future reference. Finally, clothes—we tossed Adidas, Nike, Gap, into a box for clothes to wear when we needed to clean. We needed to go shopping.

We hailed a taxi to Causeway Bay, maneuvered through the crowds of tourists, teenagers, and families, around the large shopping malls and commercial buildings, and headed to the north side of the area. Old low-rise residential buildings gave way to the sky above, and the frantic roar of the crowds faded into a soft drone a distance away. Minimalistic boutiques and shops lined the quiet streets. The demographic noticeably changed—foreigners, horn-rimmed glasses, cashmere scarves, Chelsea boots. They probably knew the couple. The area was quiet, reminiscent of an older, more beautiful version of Hong Kong in Ann Hui and Wong Kar-wai films.

We looked into the first store we saw. It was empty, with two salespeople chatting behind the counter. A small selection of pieces hung on two sides. A few pairs of jeans hung from their belt loops in the middle section. We stepped in. The salespeople stopped chatting and smiled at us. We smiled back. *Is there anything we can help you with*? One of them asked. We shook our heads. We're just looking around. The clothes were beautifully made, each piece looking as if it was waiting for its owner to retrieve it. I felt out of place in my mass-produced attire. I passed over a few pieces before coming across an off-white eyelet embroidered blouse with a scoop neck and side patch pockets. The cotton was incredibly soft. I showed my husband and he smiled at the touch. We looked for the price tag, but there was none. My husband decided on a pair of jeans. The stiff raw denim and the button fly bothered him, but he looked good. We took the two pieces to the counter. It took us a second to register the total. The salespeople didn't seem too surprised, waiting for our response. *Is everything okay?* My husband nodded, pulled out his credit card, and signed away.

What's going on with you two? A few friends asked during dinner. Nothing, we said, it's just time we moved on to better things. They laughed. Things began to fall into place. We sold the rest of our stuff and got a good price for our car. There was a buyer lined up for our old flat and the bank approved our mortgage. We bought more things—more outfits, new shoes, vintage accessories, Apple products, books for our coffee table, and jazz LPs for the phonograph.

The move was easy—we didn't have much stuff left anyways—and we were done in a day. We invited family, friends, colleagues, old classmates, anyone we could, over to our new flat. We had no time to cook, so we ordered in from various local restaurants. Everyone admired our flat. Friends thought they'd been transported to Rio, Phuket—we had never been to Rio or Phuket. Even our parents, who were initially opposed, couldn't help but compliment the flat. *The feng shui is good*, they said, looking out from the balcony into the green. *Water, mountain, wind, you have it all.* They strolled around the flat admiring the spacious kitchen, the bathroom fittings and the hardware, noticing the subtle touches.

We decided to stay in for the first few weeks. We'd put on a record, sip on some wine, and relax on the couch, gazing into the woods. We tried at first, but we gave up on cooking, so we ordered in every night—we soon knew the delivery people by their names. All in all, it was all we thought it would be, we said.

Three months after moving in, we received an email from a friend. He asked how we were doing and how we enjoyed the new flat. He then congratulated us on getting our flat featured on the cover of a design magazine. What was he talking about? He emailed back with photos of the front cover and the article.

The cover was a large photo of our living room before we moved in. Large letters spanned the bottom half of the page. *The Green Wave: why designers are switching to reprocessed, cost-efficient materials. Interview with innovative Hong Kong designer: are synthetic Chinese materials just as good? A model home—put to the test.* The article showed various shots of our flat, detailing the materials used and the cost of each. From cabinet handles to the hardwood floor, from the teak furniture to the marble counters. The writer explained that all materials in the flat were simulated and produced to look and feel exactly like their foreign counterparts at just one-tenth of the price. In the bottom corner was a photo of the young couple.

We began to examine and inspect our apartment—for cracks in the tiling, impurities in the wood, and faults in the hardware. We began knocking on the counters, listening to their reverberations, opening and closing doors swiftly, checking for creaks in the hinges, turning faucets on and off, and watching for stutters in the flow of water. We stopped inviting people over. We spent more time in the neighbourhood, eating out and taking walks. We said yes to more engagements and parties, and stayed later in the office. People would ask how our new flat was. It's fine, we'd say.

Problems began to appear. Since it was on a low floor, the flat would get incredibly humid and damp. Mould began to appear in our food, in the bathroom, and on the walls. The trees and shrubbery were nice, but kept the flat in perpetual gloom, blocking off what little sunlight would have reached the balcony. The school nearby had started the new term since we moved in, projecting school announcements and period bells reverberating throughout. The only road that reached our area, once quiet, now underwent a multi-year expansion project. Drilling went on throughout the day, including on weekends. Traffic was backed up until late at night, directing an unending stream of exhaust at our windows.

A few months later, my husband began to feel sick. It was, at first, mild. We thought it was just a cold. The doctor gave him some medicine, but it got worse. He'd wake up in the middle of the night, dizzy and out of breath, having to sit up and take a number of deep breaths before he could settle down. He took more medicine but to no avail. We went to the doctor again and explained the situation. *Do you smoke or drink?* We didn't smoke and didn't drink often. *Have you been eating healthy?* We could eat a bit healthier. *Any history of major illnesses?* Nope. *When do you feel it at its worst?* At home. *Has this happened before?* No. *Did you move recently?*

The test left columns of marks on his arm. A number of spots flared up like welts. It was called multiple chemical sensitivity. It happens when people have adverse reactions to low levels of toxic chemicals in synthetic materials. *It's not life-threatening,* the doctor said and gave us a few suggestions.

We washed and scrubbed the floors, counters, cabinets, and every surface we could. We replaced the "wooden" furniture with steel and glass designs. We installed an air purification and ionization system and replaced all the filters in our air conditioning units. We diffused aromatherapy oil throughout the day. We did all we could think of.

The flat began to reach further into our lives. We'd try to find excuses not to go home. Sometimes I'd spend an hour or two in the park waiting for my husband to get off work. Other times we'd go to the cinema for late-night showings just to get some rest. We'd be careful to keep the flat as neat as possible. Before we sleep, we'd take time to arrange whatever had been moved out of place. We'd say as little as possible about the flat as if it could hear us. Sometimes we'd whisper.

It then began to affect my husband's work. Sometimes he'd be sitting at his desk, and it'd just hit him. He'd feel sick to his stomach and would have to rush to the bathroom. He became more lethargic. Dark circles outlined his eyes and his walk slowed as if he needed to measure his ability to take the next step. He continued to have regular checkups, but there were no other problems.

I called the real estate agent and explained the situation. *What do you want me to do?* she asked. I told her about the magazine article. *You should've known: this isn't British Hong Kong anymore.* She hung up. We thought about renting the place out —what if the tenants have allergic reactions too? We thought about renovating the flat, but we were just sick of it altogether. We talked to our parents. *We told you and you didn't listen*, they said.

A month later, we signed the contract, finalizing the deal. The buyers didn't care about the interior—they were going to tear it apart anyways. We stood in the living room on the day of settlement. The real estate agent shook her head, *that's a big loss. You could've gotten more if you waited.* We handed her the keys, walked out, and shut the door behind us.

We walked down the road that had become familiar to us, past the restaurants where we ordered countless meals, past the shops, the market, the stalls, and into the city. It was rush hour. We stood on the sidewalk and watched men and women in suits and dresses crawling their way to the MTR, crowding around the bus stops, and hopping into taxis. My husband looked at me, eyes glazed over. I forced a smile and reached out to straighten his collar.

We crossed the street and entered a place once familiar to us. I ordered a number one meal, he ordered a number four meal, supersized. Two Cokes and two McFlurries. It was noisy. There were students in their uniforms studying, people in gym clothes sweaty from their post-work run, a group of elderly in the corner chatting over cups of tea and stacks of newspapers, and domestic helpers on their phones. A line of workers assembled the products with a robotic pulse—bun, patty, lettuce, ketchup, pickle, bun, and wrapper. The conveyor belt squeaked as it dropped a neatly wrapped burger into its respective receptacle. We placed our Octopus card on the reader. Beep. *Thank you. How may I help you?* the cashier said in one breath, to us, and to the man standing behind us.

We shared a large table with a couple and their kids. We unwrapped the burgers—it had been a long time. I took a bite and washed the rubbery meat down with Coke. I picked up a few fries and dropped them into my mouth. I wiped the glossy varnish off my fingertips with a napkin. My husband took a large bite out of his burger, splattering ketchup over his white Merino polo—the shirt was new. He got up and headed to the bathroom. It'd probably stain.

The two kids next to me began squirming in their seats. The mom put her index finger over her lips. *Shhh. Be quiet. Everyone's looking.* They began to complain. She put her food down and glared at her two children. The dad looked at the three of them, sighed, shook his head, and continued eating. She began to raise her voice. *Can you not hear me?* The kids paid no attention. *Stop it right now.* They began throwing their food onto the ground. A few fries landed next to my plimsolls. There was suddenly a sharp smacking sound, then, another. Heads turned. Their faint whines escalated into full-out roars. I watched as the couple grabbed their children by their wrists, yanked them out of their seats, and dragged them out the door.

My husband sat down. What happened he asked, noticing the food strewn all over the table, and debris on the ground. I don't know, I responded. I took another bite out of my burger and he did the same. But in fact, I did know, and so did he. And we wondered, as we munched on our synthetic burgers, simulated fries, and imitation ice cream, if what just happened, and what we knew, made a difference, at all.

Two Tins of Dried Smelts

by Garry Engkent

When my mother passed away and left her old house in my care, I was lost. My childhood home was to be swept of all possessions so that the place could be sold. There was so, so much musty, lingering stuff. Each dust-encrusted item held deep sentiment and deeper memories; memories of a time, of a place, of a situation. As I looked, some came immediately, some took a moment to recall, and some crept into consciousness and clarity much, much later. Then my thoughts would gush from head to heart, and I burst into deep crying.

Ahmah was not here physically anymore, but her spirit permeated everything. And I was here to remove everything. Sell it. Give it away. Toss it into a garbage bin. I was to wipe out a lifetime. Hers—and mine.

Hidden in the innermost reaches of the cold cellar shelves were two tins, one rectangular and the other circular. These containers still had faintly recognizable colourful, oriental floral designs. They must have been stored here for decades, ever since my parents and I first moved to this home. The tins had a thick coating of grey dust and cobwebs. On the top of each tin, written on strips of Band-Aid adhesives, were three rows of Chinese characters. I recognized our family name in my mother's handwriting.

I held and stared at the two tins for a very long time.

Should I open them? I did not want to desecrate anything.

I shook one of the containers. Things inside rattled. Brushing off the dust, I opened the rusted lid. Inside were desiccated smelts, little fishies, bigger than shiner minnows, but not quite the size of a sunfish or rock bass. Each was five inches long. Some had been broken up by time, or by my shaking of the oblong tin... They had the smell, not of rot and decay, but of preserved oldness.

"Everybody puts things in freezers to keep," I remembered saying then.

"Freezer cost money. No keep for long time," she replied. "Fan gwei way. Not Chinese."

Ahmah believed in the old country tradition of storing food items. "You never know when food would be scarce in famine or war," she would repeat. "Even in *Gum San*, Canada. Dried goods could keep for weeks, months, or years until needed. That's why I had your father build a cold cellar soon after we moved to this house."

I remembered the time when we went smelt fishing. It was early spring and the weather was still cold but the snow had melted. I was six and a half years old and had been in *Gum San* for about a year after my mother and I were permitted to emigrate from Hong Kong. My father was an avid fisherman in his spare time and he wanted to acquaint his son with life here in the western world. After a hard winter, he wanted to show me what spring was like.

We were going to Parry Sound, off the Georgian Bay area, some 150 miles southwest of Thibeault Falls. There would be a smelt run that week. The mature fish were ready to spawn, and my father did not wish to miss this harvest. He had been doing this annually even before WWII when a customer at the Panama Café introduced him to this sport.

"It is easier than catching pickerel or pike with a fishing rod," he said. "You just run a net in the river and scoop up the smelts. No limit on smelts. We can have bushels in less than an hour."

I nodded readily. All winter I was cooped up either in the restaurant doing chores or at school learning English. This was my first chance to get out and go somewhere, to ride for a long distance in my father's Oldsmobile.

"It's about a two-hour drive," my father informed us. "The smelt run won't really start until nine so we'll be leaving at about six. Lots of people there. Like a big party!"

"All this is done in the dark?"

"Of course. I have Coleman lanterns," my father assured her. "Use naphtha lighting, brighter than a flashlight. Can see the paths easily."

"Maybe I should come." Ahmah looked at me with worried eyes. I was the only child here in the family. She was 40 when I was born.

I was afraid that I would lose my chance at fun. Adventure. Something to contribute to the class when it was time to "Did it and Tell it." I was sure that none of my classmates had ever gone to a smelt run in Parry Sound. On a school night at that!

The smelt run in Parry Sound was an annual event that brought all sorts of people together. Some came to socialize as they would in winter ice fishing, the camaraderie, the drinking and carousing, the good times. The smell of beer and whiskey was strong and my mother commented on the rowdiness of the smelt fishermen and women.

My father had a hard time finding a spot to park the car. He muttered that we should have come earlier.

"You don't want to lug a bushel of smelts to the parking lot or even up the rocky incline," he explained. "I hope to fill five or six bushels."

"I'm strong," I said confidently.

"A bushel of wet, writhing smelts weighs more than you," he laughed. Then he started netting the mounds of smelts into bushels. I wanted to do that. Easier and faster than just fishing on the wharf.

"Be careful," my mother warned, "don't slip on the wet rocks."

With a net in hand, I scampered ahead, jostled into the crowd, and found a spot. I extended my net into the rushing waters of the river.

"This is fun!" I cheered.

And then I fell into the frigid river. I was still holding onto the pole that held the net that held a massive amount of squirming smelts. I didn't dare let go of my very first catch. I didn't dare let go for dear life. I didn't dare let go for fear of what my father would say about losing his net.

"Let go of the net, kid!" someone shouted. I did so but the strap around my wrist held on. I was pulled deeper into the river. The water was frigid. I took in a freezing mouthful. I could feel the iciness soaking into and through my boots, pants, and jacket.

I felt hands grab at my flailing arm and then a big splash. The person trying to catch me slipped and fell deep into the water. It was Ahmah. She held onto me as the other rescuers grabbed and pulled us to safety.

Ahmah was wet. I was cold and wet. My father was furious. He had wanted a few more bushels before packing up and we had ruined it for him. My mother tried to give me more warmth as she bundled me closer to her in the backseat of the car. But we were both soaking wet. We shivered together. I could smell the fresh smelts, even in the trunk of the car.

When we got back to the Café, Ahmah hustled me to the upstairs apartment and changed my wet clothes. Ahmah told me to go to bed. But once dressed in dry clothes, Ahmah and I went downstairs and unloaded the bushels of smelts, some still writhing and jumping, into the big basins. There was work to be done and the smelts just couldn't be left in the walk-in fridge. They had to be cleaned for the luncheon special the next day so she, my father, and the late-night cooks worked on the piles of smelts.

Each smelt had to be individually processed: snapping off the head with the thumb and index finger, and then pulling out the guts. There were hundreds, if not thousands, in those big bushels we brought back. Then they were washed and placed in containers and stored in the fridges.

The next morning, my mother was clearing the last bushel of smelts. This time, though, I noticed that she did not snap the heads off. Rather with a small knife, she gutted the bellies and cleared the innards. That completed, she marinated these fish in brine.

"Why are you doing that?" I asked a few days later when she drained the salted smelts from the brine.

"Dry them."

"Where?"

"On the roof," she said. "You can help."

The roof above the restaurant was flat. There was the brick chimney rattling aluminum exhaust outlets and some odd, wooden crates that somehow somebody left up there. Mainly, the roof had thick tar paper and an abundance of rough pebbles to aid drainage. Ahmah brought up some meshes and used the crates to suspend the wired meshes. Then showing me what to do, she began placing the brined smelts in rows.

"We turn them over in a few hours," she said. "Good sunlight today."

She looked up in the cloudless sky and saw a flight of seagulls and other birds. A few had the audacity to swoop down and feast on the smelts. At first, she flailed her arms about to scare away the birds but later found a wooden switch which proved to be a little more effective. But the hungry birds persisted. At the time it seemed fun so I joined in at shouting and running about the meshes, scaring the birds away. When Ahmah had to go down to do her work in the restaurant kitchen it became my chore.

In the evening, she gathered up the drying smelts and took them in small boxes down to the walk-in fridge for the night. The next morning, she spread the fish again. Her battle with the birds was constant but new obstacles came about. Flies. Some of the less brined smelts were beginning to draw all sorts of insects. In abundance.

"I hope the health department doesn't get wind of this," my father commented. It was his way of expressing disapproval.

The weather held up and the sun was strong enough that before the week was out the smelts were dried to Ahmah's satisfaction. She chose the best and used recycled tins that housed almond cookies and other Chinese pastries from Hong Kong to stack and pack the smelts. I recalled that there were more than two tins.

But today, in this storage cellar, there were just these two left. More than four decades old.

Saved for a rainy day.

Saved for a time of famine.

Saved now for—just holding on.

I looked again at the Chinese characters on the circular tin more closely. Earlier, I had assumed both tins bore only my name. This was not so. I slowly came to make out my brother's name.

Yuan.

Ahmah had left each of us a tin of dried smelts.

My ten-years older brother. My adopted brother whom I had not seen since Ahmah and I flew away from Hong Kong when I was five to come to *Gum San*, the Gold Mountain, Canada. Yuan was left behind because the Canadian government would not permit non-blood relations to join an emigrating family. We left him, according to Ahmah, in tears on the tarmac at Tak Kai Airport. A cousin held Yuan back as he cried, "Ahmah, Ahmah, don't leave me!"

He was not abandoned. Well, not totally. He was given to the care of clan relatives who received monies for his room and board. Initially, my father sent money regularly. Ahmah remained in contact with regular letters.

"We can buy papers," Ahmah suggested to my father. "Old Wong is willing to sell his for $3,000, maybe even two and a half."

What Ahmah wanted was illegal but widely practised hush-hush in the Chinese community. The document was a legal piece of paper—of a sort. In the past, the Canadian government permitted residents who returned from China to claim that during the trip they sired children, usually a son or two. In reality, the sojourners had not but that declaration was documented and the falsification on paper was "legal." This "paper son" document could be sold by the holder or on the black market for inflated sums.

"No."

"Why?" she asked. "Is it the money? I will work longer hours to pay it back."

"No."

"You don't want to do something illegal? You are afraid—"

"No."

"Then, why, husband?"

"I already have a son here."

"You were very willing for me to adopt Yuan back then."

"That was during the war. I could not return to start a family."

"Yuan is family. My son! Your son! Our son! I gave him a name. Yuan. He completed us as a family then; he completes us now."

My father broke my mother's heart that day. She never recovered. Over the years the pain of separation, of loss, of a mother abandoning a beloved child was always in her heart, in her mind, in her soul. There would be letters and occasional photographs of him in Hong Kong. He was growing into manhood without a mother. In all these pictures, Yuan bore a solemn face and sadder eyes.

As the weeks, months, and years passed, I began to remember him less and less. Yuan became a phantom brother. I heard about him only from Ahmah. He was not there when I was bullied at school. He was not there to lighten the burden of chores at the restaurant. He was not there to share in the moments of happiness, ever so few. I was forgetting him. Growing up, I thought of him ever so little.

Yuan, my brother, thought of me though. When I graduated from university he sent me a gift. A set of expensive pens, to celebrate the occasion. To him, I was still the baby brother he cherished.

"He is gone," Ahmah informed me matter-of-factly one day. Then, tears flowed down her face. She became inconsolable, almost perhaps even more so than when her husband, my father, died some years ago.

In her hands was a letter. I saw that it was a returned post. I recognized the address and my own handwriting in English. She supplied the Chinese. The envelope was unopened but scorched brown on all four corners. According to Ahmah, that was a way to inform the recipient that the addressee no longer lived there, no longer alive.

Yuan had a life of 48 years.

I had Ahmah for 38. And still did for another five.

Yuan did not.

What was his life like in Hong Kong? Did he feel happiness, even joy, for a few occasions? What would have been his life had he lived in Canada? How would that have changed all our lives?

More than loss, more than sadness, guilt and shame washed over me. I had become my father, denying a bond between Yuan and me by just not caring. I hardly ever asked my mother how Yuan was doing, what my brother was doing as he was growing up, as he was living in Hong Kong. I recalled the times that Ahmah read his letters. She held back the tears but her face and hands trembled. Things were not going well. And I kept silent, not really wanting to know.

Now here alone in a stark, cold storage room, I shed bitter tears for a brother I never really knew. I wept for my mother and for her loss. I cried for my selfish self.

Ahmah was gone.

Except for her two tins of smelts.

Should I toss the contents into the garbage bin? It was obvious that these smelts could not be kept, cooked or eaten. Or, given away.

I went to the cemetery. I dug a deep hole near the marble headstone—between the graves of my father and mother—and buried the two tins of smelts.

Closure.

So I hoped.

Over the years, there are many times when I hear dried smelts in dusty, tin boxes rattle in remembrance.

A God or Two Could Help

by Sambriddhi Nepal

The words were waiting to be needed. They gush out of me, and I'm left wondering if I believe in a god, or three million of them, after all. For so long, I had run from them, afraid of their hold on me. I had run until I had found myself, aged nineteen, lying on the floor of an apartment in Vancouver. I'm crying over a boy. My eyes are puffy, my lips are chapped, and my throat is hoarse. I am lonely in the way only a first heartbreak can make someone feel.

I plead: *He bhagwan, shakti dinus.* Oh, Lord, grant me strength.

———

My mother, her sisters, and my grandmother asked for strength all the time. The occasion didn't matter. They said it during lazy afternoons spent at my grandparents' house in Kathmandu when an afternoon downpour and the prospect of a wet, muddy rickshaw ride home was an inconvenience that required the assistance of the divine. They whispered it quietly at a family gathering when the arrival of estranged family members brought up generations of conflict. My grandmother said it loudly during a lull in the conversation, as if she needed something to ground herself, and only the gods could do that for her. Everyone needed *bhagwan*.

My father, attempting to lighten the mood, would ask if a traffic jam, a regular occurrence in the narrow, overcrowded streets of my hometown, really required one or more gods to intervene. "Do you really want to bother a god with that?" he'd say. He'd laugh, confident that his joke would land despite the frequent repetition. That was his strength.

It wasn't ever reassuring to my mother. Sitting anxiously in the passenger seat of my parent's car, she would rummage through her purse to find something that would provide momentary comfort in this unmanageable situation. She'd fish out a cough drop, or wrap herself even more tightly in her paisley-patterned shawl. Perhaps that was Parvati acting at the moment to assure her that they would get to their destination soon enough.

The incantation wasn't one I relied on. What could these gods do for me? I knew the expectations that came with being raised a woman by parents practicing conservative, Brahmin Hinduism. I didn't ask Ganesh for strength as my mother told me, aged only eleven, that my first period meant my body was changing, and that I should make sure boys didn't look at me. I didn't ask Krishna for help as she sat me down on the carpet in her bedroom three years later, her phone's handset still warm from a long conversation with her cousin, whose son had dared to marry someone non-Nepali. "If you ever do that, I'll never speak to you again," she said, her eyes ablaze. Staring at the pink flowers on her bedsheets to avoid eye contact, I didn't think there was a god anywhere who would douse that flame for me. I thought only about never becoming the match that lit it. In an instant, I became good at keeping secrets.

I didn't ask any gods for guidance on the evening I left Kathmandu to go to university in Vancouver. We didn't know it then, but I wouldn't return to Nepal again. As she prayed with a fervour I had never seen before, I sat beside my mother in her puja room, a fragrant marigold garland around my neck, red tika on my forehead, and a knot of relief and sorrow in my stomach. My right hand's fingertips were stained red from the red and orange abir and *sindhur* we'd used during the puja. They would remain that colour for a few days, traveling with me across the Pacific Ocean. I stared down at the murtis of gods and goddesses in front of me, daring them to appear and punish me. I was convinced this was my farewell to pujas.

And yet, the words found me, all those years later on my cold vinyl floor. After that first encounter, they would find me at other times. They scared me with their brazenness, the audacity to make an appearance uninvited. I kept pushing them away, but they knew I needed them.

———

For the women who raised me, being a woman was *dukha*. They lived in multigenerational homes with their in-laws, who treated them poorly and expected perfection from them. Their lives were weighed down by the pressure of being subservient daughters-in-law, generous wives, and strict mothers. They were instructed to give up or scale down careers, conduct countless religious ceremonies, and raise children who did the same. Despite this, they were pragmatic about their suffering. Long conversations recounting the hurt they had endured often ended with one of them saying, *"estai ho."* This is just the way it is. *"Ke garne?"* What can we do? There were only two things they thought they could control: their children and their prayers.

With their requests to the gods, they were showing me where to turn for comfort. They taught me I would need strength. To their horror, I found enough of it to leave. That my mother threatened me as a teenager makes sense now. She was scared for me. She was scared of me. She may have asked for the gods' help, but nothing turned up. Her threats were the only way she knew to reach me.

I have been estranged from these women for eight years. In this time, we have grieved deaths, illnesses, and natural disasters. Now, in a pandemic that has hit Nepal particularly hard, my aunt has died. Each time a tragedy has occurred, our sorrow has been a momentary closing in the chasm between us. There are short phone calls, during which tears flow freely, and silences are long and painful. The moment will pass, and the distance will return.

Grieving in estrangement relies on imagined interactions. There are no communal rituals or conversations with the people who knew my aunt best. I fill the void of lost time and missed opportunities with daydreams. I'm sure it's not always accurate, but it's all I have. Using all those afternoons in my grandparents' house as a blueprint, I dream up what my aunt and I would say to one another if we sat in a room together. A few minutes into our conversation, her booming laugh would bring her sisters and mother into the room, wanting to join in on the fun. We would talk about the most fashionable *kurthas* of the day and trade lipsticks, seeing which shades look best on each of us. A funny family anecdote would get retold, each of us shouting over the others to tell our versions. The stories are long now, new details have been added at each retelling. Inevitably, the conversation would transition to family dynamics. Old wounds and disappointments would resurface. Someone in the room would bring up *dukha*, and I'd ask where my aunt sought solace. She'd say she found it in puja, in *bhagwan*, in doing what she had to do. *Estai ho*.

———

73

Today, there isn't an altar or a murti near me in my home. I close my eyes. Before the tears come I ask for strength. For me, and for the women I love and resent. I'm closer to them than I had thought.

Daisies and Polka Dots

by Saya Watanabe

Obaachan arrives in Canada for the first time on a sparkling August day, during the last two weeks of summer vacation. Inside the airport, the air-conditioning sends goosebumps up my arm and I gaze out the window at the wispy clouds, wishing I were at Lina's party, eating Cheetos and reading the Seventeen magazines we stole from her sister's bedroom. Standing next to me, my mom squints up at the Arrivals bulletin again before scanning the crowd that filters out the corridor. I follow her gaze, landing on a flight attendant standing near the bathroom. She has the longest brown hair that curls in just the right places, and I fidget, pulling at my own hair, stick straight and stubborn as ever.

"Can't I just play Nintendo in the car?" I grumble and start picking at my dress. It's covered in frilly lace. Very Japanese. I hate it. Obaachan mailed it to us last winter, forgetting that I was already ten, and it makes my arms look like pink sausages.

"You want heatstroke?" My mom shoots me her death glare and

peers across the airport. "And what did I say about speaking Japanese from now on? Obaachan doesn't understand English."

I roll my eyes, pretending to slump over on the bench. "What's the point? She's not even here yet."

"Look, look, I think I see her!" Waving like a maniac, my mom pulls me onto my feet.

"Where?" I don't recognize anybody in the crowd of suitcases and excited families. The last time I saw Obaachan was three years ago when we visited my mom's hometown in Gifu-ken. I barely remember anything besides the noisy cicadas and the plane ride that made me so sick I threw up six times. Though my mom called Obaachan a few times a month, to me, she was just a face in photographs and a voice that would ask how I was doing in Japanese school.

Suddenly, my mom rushes over to hug a woman wearing a daisy-patterned shirt and polka dot pants that clash loudly. She kind of looks like my Obaachan, but shrunken, and I hesitate until she reaches out and squeezes me with a hug. "Yui-chan, you've grown so big," she says in a voice so loud that it causes the couple next to us to turn and stare. I hear our words, harsh and alien, grating against the English that flows smoothly through the space like music.

"Hi, Obaachan," I mumble.

"You look so beautiful," she says, patting me on the head. "I remember how much you love princesses, so when I saw this dress, I knew you would love it. Look at how perfect it fits." The sleeves itch, and I yank them down, unsure of what to say. But then Obaachan' face curves into a smile so wide I can see her molars, and I think I remember her again, so I grin back, toothy and childish too.

My mom gathers up Obaachan's suitcases, gesturing toward the exit. "Let's head to the car. How was the flight, Mom? Did you get through customs okay?" Her face is pink with excitement. They start walking ahead, launching into peals of laughter as I follow, feeling my shoes squeak against the floor.

———

A week into Obaachan's trip, my mom drops us off at Zeller's while she runs errands. After days of stuffy car rides to Grouse Mountain and Lynn Canyon, I race through the doors, leaving Obaachan to trail behind as I skid down the accessory aisle. Spotting the display, I screech to a stop. The row of shiny hair extensions, all colors of the rainbow, hangs just out of reach.

"Yui-chan, you run so fast," Obaachan pants, rounding the corner. She closes her eyes and launches into another one of her stories. "When you came to Gifu, I remember how you would run all through the house and stomp your feet across the tatami floors..."

I tune out the sound of her voice and focus on the extensions, brushing my fingertips through the silky hair and imagining what it would look like. Last week, when I met Lina at the swimming pool, her long hair was scrunched into a baseball cap. Once I pointed it out, she dramatically swept off the hat, letting strands of dyed hair tumble loose. She looked like Avril Lavigne, swirls of pink mixed into her honey-blond locks. "Wow," was all I could say. "It's actually just Kool-Aid," she giggled. "But my mom's gonna take me to the salon before school starts."

Just then, Obaachan taps me on the shoulder and I spin around. "Yui-chan," she whispers like she has a secret. "Your Obaachan will buy you a gift."

"Really?" I wrap my arms tightly around her waist, feeling her laughter thunder from deep in her belly. She hugs me back. "Choose any toy you want."

Toys are lame, for babies, but I gaze up at the extensions again, torn between the options. Purple, the colour of grape Fanta, catches my eye. "This one," I announced to Obaachan, waving the package over my head. Light with giddiness, I skip ahead to the cash register.

It's quiet in the store, no line, and the only open cashier is an older man, hunched over a sudoku puzzle. He looks up as I walk over, blue eyes studying me. "Are you Japanese?" he asks, smiling at me. "Konnichiwa?"

I freeze in the middle of placing the extensions on the counter, staring at him like a deer in the headlights, cheeks burning hot. *Hi*, I want to say. *Hi, hi, hi, hi, hi.*

He tries again. "Konnichiwa?" At that moment, I hear Obaachan shuffle up behind me, wheezing slightly. "Konnichiwa!" she answers, delighted.

The man beams. "I could tell you aren't Korean. Or Chinese," he says proudly, in stilted Japanese. "You know, I lived in Japan for a year in my twenties. I still study the language when I can."

"Your speaking skills are very good," Obaachan exclaims.

"Are you here," the man pauses, struggling to remember the right word. "Um...on vacation?"

She nods. "It's my first time in Canada. Everyone is so welcoming," she says, plucking a twenty-dollar bill from her wallet. I snatch up the extensions.

The man rips off the receipt with a flick of his wrist, smiling at me. "I hope you two have a nice visit. Sayonara!" *She's the visitor,* I want to say. *Not me.* But the words stick in my throat like a ball of chewing gum.

"Sayonara," Obaachan replies, and I storm away.

When we reach the store entrance, Obaachan tugs on my sleeve until I stop walking. "Yui-chan, is everything okay?" I stare into her weathered face. She blinks at me, unaware, and I swallow my shame, wanting to disappear. Wanting *her* to disappear. "Why did you have to follow me here?" I say, fists clenched. "Why did you have to speak to that man in Japanese?" My words splinter in the air and then it's too late to take it back, too late to apologize as I leave her behind.

———

The car ride home is filled with a cool silence and the hiss of the air-conditioning. I rip open the package, holding up strands of purple hair and admiring how they shimmer in the sunlight. My mom glances back and notices. "What is that?"

"Obaachan bought me extensions," I brag, waving them around.

"You spoil her," my mom frowns at Obaachan, before turning back to me. "For your hair? Won't teachers get mad?"

I roll my eyes, carefully clipping in the extensions. "Everyone at school uses *actual* dye, Mom."

Obaachan smiles at me. "I like your natural hair. The colour of nori, like mine used to be."

"Black is boring, Obaachan."

My mom makes a face at her and shrugs. "I guess it's popular with gaijin," using the term for foreigners.

"Yui is not a gaijin..." Obaachan insists, but then her voice wavers when she peers into my face, as if she is looking at me for the first time. Ignoring her frown, I comb my fingers through the strands, feeling a shiver of excitement as I turn to look at my reflection in the mirror.

Instead of blending into a smooth ombre, the extensions stick together in synthetic sections. My hair is too dark, and the purple is too bright, clashing like a cheap Halloween costume. Like daisies and polka dots. The car rolls over a bump and a wave of nausea rocks my stomach as I yank out the extensions and stare at the black strands that also fall out, biting my lip so hard I taste blood.

In the side mirror, I look at Obaachan's reflection. From the backseat, she is close enough for me to reach forward and touch the silver hairs that poke through the headrest. We share the same eyes, dark brown like coffee, I realize, and I hold my breath, waiting to catch her gaze so she can see the silent apology etched in mine. But she just stares out at the landscape of trees and mountains that swim by in a big green blur. Instead, I lean my head on the window and gaze outside, too. The sky is pure, like Kool-Aid blue. In the distance, a plane glides through the sky, and I envy its ease, the way it navigates the big open space between here and there.

LITTLE MEN

BY RACHEL ABELINDE

The stone remained cold and silky gray in the boy's palm.

He was in the middle of a procedure that many in the village had seen performed and found nothing spectacular about. Yet he sat on the bamboo steps of the hut in rapture, eyes bright with the idea that at any time a sort of magic was to take place, and his palm, with the cold gray stone, would be the central point of its demonstration.

Set on experiencing the unnatural, he absent-mindedly used his free arm to lock his older cousin's elbow into an anchor with his own. The older cousin, a girl, was herself amused at what was unfolding: here was an eager, clueless child by her side; an elderly healer in front of them, murmuring what might be a prayer in earnest, and their aunties, fidgeting and fanning themselves to fend off the heat. It was only the sun at midday, but this mild deviation from their normal worked quite a discomfort on the two women. They kept their worried eyes on the boy—he who, the night prior, told his older cousin about his unusual little men friends.

————

"There were two types," he said, the evening having barely touched the tiny space that made up their entire kitchen. "The first one," he commenced, "only wanted to play under the stairs" – their old rickety stairs at the house he grew up in in the Visayas – "favoring small toys, especially colourful marbles."

"The second, sinister type," he added, waving his finger, "would, after a game, offer you food in the wrong colour, like rice in black or water in a dark blue." It was this second type that constantly urged you to go home with them.

His older cousin, who was tinkering with the stove handle, paused before interjecting: "You mean you were playmates with a *duwende* on several occasions?" The boy confirmed this but clarified that it was not just *a duwende* but a handful of them, never mind that they showed up erratically, with varying energy, and dressed so alike it was possible he had counted one many times over.

As for the rules: never gloat when, in your games, you find yourself on a winning streak (the little men disliked having their friendly losses rubbed in), refuse all food politely, and decline every invitation to accompany them home. If you gave in, well, you were never sure you could return – that much he knew. So be stern in your refusal. And if they keep pressing this point, it wouldn't be wrong to threaten them with ending the friendship altogether.

But, the boy went on, the last he saw of these friends was in the driest of summers, before he was taken here up north to where their aunts lived, on that excruciatingly long trip by bus "for a vacation," as he was told then.

He remembers, though, and this he relayed to his cousin evenly, barely hinting at how he felt, that his mother, who worked in a teaching assistant post in the Middle East, was set to return around this time of year to their own home in the province – so why was he here, so far from where his mother would have wanted him to be?

Oil crackled violently as his older cousin placed a slab of tilapia into the skillet.

She couldn't tell him what she and the aunties already knew: that his mother had stopped communicating with the family. A few weeks back, they received word that she had given birth abroad, to a chinky-eyed multiracial bundle – if the stories were true, and how quaint that they relied mostly on rumours still.

It had been over eighteen months since she left the country. "For my son," she said back then, adding that perhaps, with some luck, she'd be able to send for him so the two of them could start over, eventually, as Canadians or Australians or whatever the appellation for wherever would be the most suitable place to move to later on. Husbandless and so very young, no one at that time doubted her grit – no one wanted to – until she grew elusive online and stopped sending funds for the boy's upkeep.

"Can't I say it out loud?" one of the aunties said as the other shook her head and sunk her chin in defeat. "The girl's a *disgraciada* through and through."

There it was then, judgment pronounced – after holding back on labelling her for years. The aunties declared too that there was no use arguing their kin's fitness for motherhood. The clueless child, who crossed the San Bernardino Strait on board a ferry, assaulted by sea and wind, and who after that, traversed several towns of the Bicol region by bus before reaching the aunts in Southern Tagalog, had for them been rendered necessarily motherless; *this* compounded by the fact that his father up to this day remained unknown and unnamed. By default then, the childless aunties in the family could claim him as their own.

When he arrived, unkempt and needlessly shy, they looked at him as much with love as with pity, with a nervous expectation that he would approve of them too. They wound their arms around the boy, as if to tell him they would protect and nurture him from there on in.

The boy smiled and smiled as the women fussed and gleamed, trying his utmost not to appear worn down. But later in his sleep there would be the sea spray, blotting the window of the ferry's air-conditioned inner deck as his tiny body retched and tumbled from seasickness.

At dinner, the older cousin told the aunts the boy's story about his so-called little men friends.

Now, these elderly women were clear-headed even in a crisis. They had heard of these stories from their hometown, of *duwende* befriending – sometimes abducting – children. And though the aunties were modern city dwellers now, they never quite developed a conceit against traditional healing, which they thought of as the first line of defence in these situations. Hence, the following day, all four of them set out for the western coast. From there, they took a *banca* to the healer's village across the bay.

And that was how the motherless boy, friend to little creatures and believer in magic, ended up ensconced in the healer's humble residence.

There were other children milling about the hut too, and rarely with a complete set of clothing. It seemed they preferred to walk around without slippers – liked, perhaps, how sand felt on bare, tiny feet. They were as raucous as the little boy was solemn, and very easily given to laughter.

As the procedure in the boy's palm progressed, with the healer's murmurs turning into audible syllables, mothers came one by one to pick the children up, whisking them home for lunch and scolding them for carousing, telling them off for discarding their clothes and slippers. The sun was too high up, they said. Not the time to be out and about and careless.

By this time, the healer had plucked the stone from the boy's palm. With a mallet, she crushed the pebble into fine powder. She then took out a thin, pliable metal like a razor blade, used it to make a swift, shallow cut just under the boy's thumb, and slid some powder into the bloodless sliver of skin, as neatly as one would a handkerchief into a pocket.

The idea was to have the consecrated particles act as a talisman against the supernatural. "Don't worry too much now," the healer entreated. The boy, she said, will be safe from seeing and being seen by those who aren't like us – the ones the aunts referred to as *"mga ginlabog han gino-o,"* creatures whom God threw away.

The older cousin, meanwhile, assured herself that the cut was, thankfully, too superficial to risk infection. And despite her doubts, she sincerely hoped this would work. She had lived with the aunties long enough to understand how they willingly teetered between past and present, and how their pragmatism was such that if the boy later on claimed that he could still see his little friends, the women were just as likely to see another spiritualist as they would a psychologist, if they could afford it.

Before he came to see the aunts, the boy thought, mornings meant rising to an *adlaw*, not a sun, and on warm nights he would run around in his slippers playing tag with other children under a *bulan* – prior to calling it the moon.

When this, his adoptive tongue, was introduced to him – to prepare for his new school, the aunts said, where students are asked to speak only English – he had already learned at home the languages of the Pacific gods, the way his mother did. The aunts sometimes spoke in the vernacular too, but not as easily as his mom.

Another memory: of mosquito nets and petrol lamps, his mother, graceful and kind, whisking the air rhythmically with a woven fan, keeping him cool as they lay on a sleeping mat one humid evening. She liked to sing to him a – "Here before we head back," he heard the younger auntie call out as the *banca* came to a halt and he was jolted to the here and now.

They were taking a different route back, so this stop was a curiosity for the boy. The older women disappeared into a row of wooden structures baking neatly under the sun, perhaps on some errand he had failed to catch as he daydreamed.

"Lemery," his cousin volunteered. They saw that this town did not have the yellowish sand of other beaches. Rather, sediments of black ran the length of the shore. Now and again, waves bathed the sand in seawater, leaving behind a rich black pudding. Only in parts not reached by the water was the sand loose and an uneven gray.

His cousin told him that there really were no white sand beaches in this part of the country. The beaches in nearby areas, so advertised for their near-whiteness, merely had layers of light-colored sand gouged from elsewhere, possibly the islands to the south, which were poured over Batangas's black shores.

They were standing on authentic, unprettified sand then; a welcome and unassuming contrast to the water that in the distance spread into the silvery blue sea. The boy tried removing his slippers, but at half past two in the afternoon, with the sun well above the horizon, he found soon enough that the sand was too hot to walk on barefoot.

Why haven't the aunties returned, the older cousin wondered. And, out loud, "Probably saw something they liked and are still haggling with a vendor now."

At this, a query lingered on the boy's face. "Do you think this," he held out his palm, "will still work when I get home?"

She paused to consider what the question implied. "You mean you still want to see the little men?"

"With the aunties, well, I have to be polite. But I never wanted my friends gone."

She understood now how all throughout no one had asked this hopeful, confident child.

What she would like to do was return to the *banca* and sit on one of the wooden outriggers. She would dip both feet into the water, slice the surface with her ankles, and watch the water foaming in swathes.

The boy, on the other hand, stared out, content, mesmerized by the vast horizon; he was thinking what it would be like to ride on the back of a cloud.

OCEAN BOY

BY CARLA CRUJIDO

Late one night, before summer turned to fall, Ocean Boy was born in a desert town at the confluence of two mythic rivers. He was descended from men who dove for pearls in the waters of a faraway Pacific archipelago, fished the deep waters off the coast of the city named after a saint. His mother was a girl who could dive deeper and swim faster than the boys of her one-time coastal town. A mermaid, the kind ones called her. Bottom dweller, the unkind ones said.

As he grew from a boy to a man, he played the guitar to keep the demons of despair that haunted him at bay. Wrote songs of longing for a place that sang to him as he slept. Plaintive baleful songs soaked with melancholy. Songs of the deepest blue. But here, in this town at the river's edge—where the winds were fierce and dust could blind—his songs fell on ears that could not hear the rhythm of the ocean written into them.

Ocean Boy started to spin in the chaos of winds called Relocation. He could not breathe. The doctors called it asthma but his mother knew it was homesickness for the home he had not yet found. The one that saturated his songs and him.

The days passed and the music that once flooded him stopped. Perplexed by the loss of his lifelong companion, he put down his guitar.

"What are you doing?" his mother asked.

"I can't hear anything but the wind. The music is gone," he said. "Dead. Who am I without it?"

"You are your music," she said.

"Exactly," he said.

He thought of his grandpa who lived and died because of these winds, this town, that power plant. The winds blew men off the job site—away from home, away from marriages, away from children. The leaving winds. His grandpa had chosen to stay.

"I gave everything to that company," he would remind. The edges of his grandpa glowed green when the sun set. Did he have death scripted into his DNA like his grandpa, because of his grandpa?

Ocean Boy moved to the city that was emerald. Went to work in a restaurant in Nihonmachi owned by a childhood friend of his grandpa's. Washed dishes until the old man pulled him into the kitchen.

"Enough," he said one night. Instead, he trained him to slice vegetables, cut fish, hand press vinegar rice. Ocean Boy took pride in his work. He wanted to prove himself, show the old man he could do it—for himself and his grandpa. He practiced, perfected.

"Very good, very good," the old man praised.

On days when Ocean Boy didn't work, he wandered the streets of his neighbourhood. He liked that it was once known as the Lava Beds. Thought it fitting since his family hailed from a strand of islands with one hundred volcanoes. He also liked that these blocks were once the centre of the city's vice and sin—brothels, box houses, saloons and gambling halls—which, he thought, always made a place or a person more interesting. He drank beer in a tavern with one hundred years of sordid stories soaked into its floorboards, ate tacos on a patio facing an alley filled with art and bantered with a beautiful server named after a song, searched for ghost signs on the sides of old brick buildings. Sometimes, he sat under the viaduct and smoked cigarettes as he watched the late afternoon light flirt with the water of Elliott Bay.

"Sit," the old man said one night after the restaurant emptied. "Tonight, we celebrate Ebisu, the happy god of children, fish, and fortune. I want to make you something special."

He pulled up his sleeve, chased a blowfish with a net, scooped it from the tank, leaned in and said something to it. Quickly and deftly moved his knife through the fish until it became whispers of sea flesh mounded on a plate with white radish and green citrus. He poured cold rice wine into a cup, pushed it across the short expanse of glass. Raised his own bottle of beer to Ocean Boy.

"Kanpai!" each said to the other.

"What did you say to him?" asked Ocean Boy.

The old man laughed, "I told him not to kill you. Fugu is very poisonous if not cut correctly."

Five nights a week, Ocean Boy and the old man sat on crates in the alley and smoked cigarettes. Sometimes they talked, sometimes they sat in silence. The old man looked forward to this time, so did Ocean Boy. It began with small talk: What did you do on your day off? Have you tried the malasadas at Fuji? The barbecued pork at Tai Tung? Did you catch the game last night? The news?

Once Ocean Boy tried to ask the old man about his time working side by side with his parents in the fields of the Sacramento Delta, his childhood internment at Topaz. Two particular things he knew about him.

"Forgotten time," he said. But Ocean Boy knew a childhood sliced in two by toil and war was not forgotten.

"Tell me your stories," the old man said. So he did.

He told him how he grew up in a loving, left-of-centre family: mom, grandma, grandpa, an auntie, two uncles. How food and laughter were their religion. How beyond their small circle life was a series of small and large cruelties and that over time, they became tidal, threatened to drown. How the children called him Whale. A single word taunt stuck on repeat, followed by peals of laughter that shadowed him to the cafeteria, the gym, the library. When he was older and the roundness of childhood had dropped away, the jibe turned to *Thinks he's Neptune,* sneered with derision. How his grandpa had died before he had taught him how to be a man. Before they had gotten to take long road trips together that would involve burgers eaten at roadside stands and winning numbers inked onto Keno paper.

"We'll win big, his grandpa said. Move to the islands. I'll paint and you can play music. We can fish and go kau kau."

But the poison that was nuclear took him too soon.

Ocean Boy told the old man how his father—whose ancestors came from an island in a sea where selkies swam—had left him behind. Set off to the Rose City to make the dreams of a girl not much older than Ocean Boy come true. When their ill-fated love affair reached its expiration date, he was lured in by a woman of the land: tall and strong and thick as the trees that lined the shores of the river that cut their metropolis in two. He became a footnote in his father's story. Forgotten when the new wife had one child, then two.

He was erased.

He told of how he put down his guitar when a sound void hit him like a tsunami. How he was assailed with an unfathomable loneliness for a place he could not name. The old man knew no advice could ease the deep ache of a life disrupted by cruelty, the inhumanity of others. He let the boy talk and he listened.

Weeks passed. Ocean Boy's memories got louder, started to loop. A sudden swell of sadness overtook him. The oceanic one he had inherited from his mother and his grandfather. The voices of the past became a reprise.

One night he touched the tip of the knife used to prepare the blowfish to the centre of his bottom lip. It tingled, numbed. A week later, he touched it to the tip of his tongue. The sensation was more intense: tingle, numb, float. He repeated it nightly. Let the knife rest longer. The fleeting thrill became a need.

Days bent into months. He died small deaths daily, heart cell by heart cell. The blowfish poison dulled the pain, dulled his dreams. At night, he fell into a chasm of black slumber or didn't sleep at all. He became disoriented, vacant, a ghost.

On nights he didn't put the Fugu knife to his lips, he'd wake the next morning with the taste of sugar and pineapple on his tongue. On the days when there was a respite from the thrum of rain inside his head and the static of sadness went silent, he could hear the mele of the islands. *Come home*, they sang.

As the months collected into a year, Ocean Boy devoted his life to Fugu. At work, he watched the blowfish swim in their tank, whispered kind words before he took their life, sliced them, and served them. At midnight, he walked down Jackson to his apartment that sat in the night glow of Smith Tower. Turned the TV on and the sound down, opened the foil packet that held the Fugu liver stolen from the restaurant, shaved off a piece with the hand-forged Japanese knife he bought from the overpriced kitchen store at the Market, lifted it with chopsticks, placed it on his tongue, waited for the poison to surge through him. The rush of euphoria built until he thrashed and flailed, hit his head on the countertop and the underside of the cupboards, tore at the skin he wanted to escape until blood painted his nails. He gasped for air, his movements slowed, his eyes clouded. Finally, he fell into the chair in front of the mute television, his nightly ritual complete. He had become the Fugu—pulled from his tank, slapped onto the counter, skinned and sliced, devoured

Late one November night, the old man put his hand on Ocean Boy's wrist and pressed it into the cutting board before he could lift the knife to his tongue.

"I can't stop," Ocean Boy said.

The old man took the knife from his hand. You're drowning. It's time to go.

He reached into the pocket of his worn blue jacket, and pulled out a ticket. Printed in black was the island of Ocean Boy's grandpa, his great-grandpa. Ocean Boy shook his head. It's too much! The old man motioned to the other side of the counter, then joined him.

"Let me tell you a story. When your grandpa and I were little, we went to a school for Chinese, Japanese, and Filipinos only. No white kids. They had their own school. Then Pearl Harbour was bombed and we Japanese were sent to the camps. Half the children and teachers from our school disappeared, so it closed. Your grandpa and all of the others who were left were sent to the other school, the white one. When I came back after the war, the kids made my life hell—they spit on me, called me names, beat me up—even the ones I grew up with in the pear orchards and the asparagus fields. They didn't want to be close to me for fear that my misfortune was contagious. But not your grandpa, he put up his fists and fought for me. We were eleven years old. He did that for me, I want to do this for you."

It was the most the old man had ever shared.

"Take it," he said. "Please."

Ocean Boy hugged the old man and cried into the blue of his jacket.

That night, Ocean Boy packed his waterside life into two duffle bags, then called his mother.

"I get in before daybreak," he said. He got on a midnight bus and headed east across the state. Stared at his reflection in the black of the window. He was a stranger, even to himself.

His mother arrived early, but the bus arrived earlier. She circled the inside of the depot but could not find her son. On her third orbit, she stopped in front of a man: bearded, gaunt, haunted, lips cracked, a gash caked with blood over his right eyebrow.

"Ocean Boy?"

"Mama!"

In a decades-old diner, over eggs and toast and coffee, Ocean Boy described his daily escape to her as diving into blue and staying under to the moment before surrendering to the silence. But before the dive, there was the excitement that preceded the slice of body into water: the shiver, the sting, the surge.

"I'm sorry I'm so broken," he said. Salt collected on his cheekbones and hers.

A string of weeks later, he picked up his guitar, blew the dust from its neck, strummed until it became a melody. His unused voice cracked. He took a breath, reached into the hidden place inside of himself that the sadness hadn't touched. His voice grew, regained, redoubled. His mother watched as the posturing of self-preservation cracked and fell to the floor.

"You're back," she said. Her voice flooded with astonishment.

"I'm back," he said. Leaned his guitar against the wall. "But where did I go?" he asked. His seawater eyes alight with wonder. "Why didn't you save me?"

"I tried. Only you could save you."

Night after night, Ocean Boy heard a far away song as he slept. A sugared voice, a ukulele. When he opened his eyes the last notes of the song were fading as the sun pushed over the edge of the eastern sky.

One December morning, Ocean Boy stood with his mother in their tiny tri-city airport, not wanting to say goodbye. She pulled at her lower lip with her teeth. He knew she was trying to keep from crying. To keep from saying the things she really wanted to say, like, *Don't go.*

"Last call for flight," the announcement overhead bellowed.

"That's me, Mama. I've gotta go or I'll miss the plane."

"I know," she said in a voice so small it sounded like a child's.

He picked up his bag and his guitar, then leaned down and kissed her forehead. When he turned around to holler a final farewell, he saw a wave of tears crashing against her ankles.

Ocean Boy flew over the blue expanse of sea. When he arrived on the island, he checked into a hotel where Elvis stayed. This he did for his mother. He walked the streets of Chinatown. This he did for his great-grandpa. He ate burgers and fished from an old seawall. This he did for his grandpa. He sat on the beach, played his guitar, listened to the waves argue with the sand. This he did for himself. He rented a jeep and drove around the island. Made up stories of what his time with his grandpa would have looked like here. Pointed out places they should have seen together: the base where his grandpa was once stationed, the dock where his great-grandpa got off the boat from his own island, the now empty buildings where his mom used to buy shave ice and crack seed. Small histories that made up a larger one—his.

On the day before he was scheduled to fly back to the mainland, Ocean Boy stopped at a diner for eggs and rice and sausage. After he had eaten and paid the check, he stood in the parking lot and smoked a cigarette. Let the island's chords wash over him. The multisyllabic crash of the waves, the whisper and sigh of the palm trees, the velvet winged flap of the wind, the soft shoe rhythms of the late morning rain. It was, he realized, the sound of home.

She left as if she never came

by Ling Ge

Trigger warning: Contains depiction or discussion of violence and death.

It's been a year since COVID-19 restrictions prevented Minhua Zhang from leaving the Lis' house in North York. Tears welled in her eyes and trickled down her skinny cheeks as she stared at the blood glucose meter in the kitchen. She no longer wanted to live like how she had lived in the past. She discontinued her high school education as an international student to marry the Lis' ne'er-do-well son in exchange for a betrothal gift. She did it for her parents. They kept pressuring her to give them a return on their investment for her education in Canada. The Lis were good to her at first but after she gave birth to Sam last year, they've only let her eat their leftovers, and now she has developed low blood sugar. She couldn't take it anymore. She wanted to leave.

"I'm going to call the police if you keep treating me like this!" Minhua yelled in a fit of rage and threw down her apron and ran downstairs to the basement. She was going to retrieve her grammar notes and figure out how to go back to school.

Minhua's yell lingered in the dining room where Mr. Li's thoughts flashed back to his graduate supervisor. He looked at Mrs. Li and James who became still and stood aghast. They were in the middle of adjusting Sam onto his high chair.

"She's reached her limit. It's about time we get rid of her." Mr. Li rolled his chair towards his laptop on the dining table. Through networking and hypocrisy, he had obtained a full-time economics faculty position at the University of Toronto. He had learned that the easiest way of obtaining justice was by taking advantage of other naive, kind, and weak people. He deeply believed in life that the end always justifies the means.

Mrs. Li sat down to listen. James stared at his father. "How?"

"She's in the basement now. There are no windows there and we can lock the door from outside. She'll die without food and water. We'll turn off the heat too. It's the perfect time to act. We'll say that she died from COVID-19 during self-isolation." Mr. Li turned on his laptop and started punching in his credentials, "James, check if Minhua's cell phone is still in your bedroom. If so, go and lock the basement door from outside."

"What if – "

Mr. Li cut him off and pointed at the bedroom, "Just do what I say quickly before she leaves the basement. I'll explain later."

James scurried anxiously and flew to the bedroom, but then flew back with excitement. "Mom, Dad, that stupid girl left her cellphone in the room." Mr. and Mrs. Li nodded to give the go-ahead, and James tiptoed downstairs.

Minhua turned on the lights inside the basement, and found her notes within boxes of unfinished school work. She started flipping through them and smiled when she found Jennifer's contact card bookmarked between the pages. Jennifer was her high school tutor and has been the only person who has ever cared about her.

Boom, the door shut with a deafening bang.

Minhua jumped, startled. She turned towards the door and saw it closed. She quickly ran to the door knob. It wouldn't budge. It was locked. There was no wind. She stood still as it dawned on her that someone had locked her in. Again and again she pulled forcefully at the knob. Her hands hurt. She was petrified with fear. Was it because I said I'd call the police? She looked around, several boxes placed against the walls, no escape in sight. "Open the door! Open the door!" She kept knocking and screamed on top of her lungs.

James tiptoed back into the dining room. "Dad, what if someone performs an autopsy?"

While he searched for the closest cremation service, Mr. Li patiently explained to his son as if he was lecturing his students, "When a family member dies of illnesses in Ontario, without obvious trauma, an autopsy is not needed. We can get her cremated right away by sending in two forms to the funeral home. I'll ask my colleague to sign her Medical Certificate of Death indicating COVID as the cause of death." He was confident that Dr. Thomas, the family physician who had just joined his research team, would help him.

"What if her parents ask?" James frowned.

Mrs. Li smirked. "That's easy. Just like our betrothal gift, money will silence them." She went into the kitchen and brought out their green onion pancakes. "It's time to eat."

James saw his parents' confidence and felt calmer. He sat down and busied himself with feeding Sam.

The Lis took turns to make sure that the door remained locked for the next ten days. It was music to their ears when the sounds downstairs gradually decreased to nothing. On the eleventh day, Mr. Li emailed the Medical Certificate of Death to Dr. Thomas and called him, "Hello Dr. Thomas, I'm looking forward to meeting you in-person soon. Listen, I need your help. My daughter-in-law died from COVID-19 during self-isolation. It's been very difficult for me and my family. I've filled out her Medical Certificate of Death and emailed it to you. Could you immediately sign it and send it back to me so I can submit it to the funeral home? We want to get this over with as soon as possible so that we don't have to prolong the suffering."

"Hello Professor Li," Dr. Thomas hesitated, "I'm very sorry for your loss. I would be happy to help...but I never knew that she had gotten COVID-19."

"I swabbed her with my testing kit." Mr. Li responded with as grave of a voice as he could muster, the same voice he was known to use to terminate research partnerships. "Do you not trust me?"

Dr. Thomas stuttered. "Of course, I trust you. Okay. I just got your email. I'll sign it now."

"Thanks Dr. Thomas. See you later." Mr. Li said and hung up his phone. Dr. Thomas's email arrived, and Mr. Li forwarded it with the Statement of Death to York Cemetery and Funeral Home. They operated twenty-four hours a day, every day, and he called them right away.

"We want to use your cremation services. My daughter-in-law died of COVID-19 during self-isolation. I've sent to your email the Medical Certificate of Death and Statement of Death. Can you help us get a burial permit? We want to get her body out of our house as soon as possible. It's bad luck."

The representative on the line confirmed, "Yes, I see your email. I'm sorry for your loss, and I understand. We'll send the forms to the City Clerk's Office right away for a burial permit. They usually issue it within the same day. I'll ask the Funeral Director and his assistants to come to your place as soon as possible."

Mr. Li hung up and smiled. Mrs. Li and James were on standby waiting for his orders. "It's time to open the basement door."

"Mom, I'm scared." James's voice shook and grabbed onto Mrs. Li's arms.

"Don't worry. We'll go together." Mrs. Li said and went downstairs with Mr. Li. She had in her arms a quilt and a pillow. James took Sam who was sleeping and went back into his bedroom and closed the door.

Mr. Li unlocked the basement door and held his breath. He braced for the smell of a putrid odor oozing through the doorway, which briefly stopped him and Mrs. Li from entering. Yet, nothing blocked the door when he pushed, nor was there any body lying behind it. He pushed the door wider and did not see a lifeless body sprawled on top of a pile of papers on the floor as he had imagined.

Mrs. Li dropped her quilt and pillow and covered her mouth. She had prepared to cover the corpse with the quilt and slip a pillow under Minhua's head in a way that made it look like she was sleeping. Mr. Li's meticulous plan to dispose of Jennifer's notes and toss them into the garbage did not happen. He ran his hands across the walls of the tiny room and found no traces of escape. He knelt down and picked up a white envelope addressed to the Lis. Still in a daze, he slipped it into his pocket to read later.

The doorbell rang. The Funeral Director and his assistants arrived in hazmat suits. The Li family froze in time, not knowing whether to answer the door or hide. The bell rang again which woke the baby. Mr. Li suddenly felt his own words echo in his own head, "naive, kind, and weak people." His hands reached for his pocket but was afraid of what he would find in it. Minhua left as if she never came.

Can I help you, Sir?

by Klaus Tan

My clothes are my first line of defence. Matching the local style is an easy form of security. Safe from prying eyes and too many questions. Dressing up like this is not paranoia when it deals with an actual threat. No one would be able to pick me out as an oddity right away. It's added protection. It would be dumb not to wear a bulletproof vest in an active conflict, right? On second thought, that idea doesn't sit well with me. Do I really feel so threatened by a shopping mall that I consider it like walking through a warzone?

"Can I help you, sir?"

These words frighten me. Standing in front of me is a young woman dressed in the department store's uniform. Her clothing and the store itself seem more suited for the First Class cabin of an overnight flight than a shopping centre in a suburb. Her outfit matches the high-end business fashion that flight attendants around the world wear, evoking similar questions about its design practicality. A uniform crafted to fit the most luxurious cultural standards, only giving the barest lip service to cultural identifiers. The extravagant goods around her looked like products in an airplane catalogue. Watches that tell you how much money you've lost per hour and scents that tell people you have means without even looking. The most expensive items you have ever seen, available even when you're far away from Paris and London. Things people globally seem to want and which they desire to afford more than anything else.

The building has the unmistakable feel of air conditioning commonly found in such handcrafted environments. It hurts bitterly to recognize that the comfort of A/C feels more familiar to me than this whole country's ecosystem.

The young woman's smile reads like a professional habit rather than a genuine expression. Is she questioning me because it's how they greet their customers? Or did she pick me out because I seem suspicious? Does she work by commission? Do they even allow people to work by commission in this country? Her expression betrays nothing but friendliness. Regardless of why she chose to speak to me, she is my problem now. I dread this deeply.

I cannot bring myself to answer her. While I fully understand her language, there is no way of answering her without giving myself away. And yet, not answering at all would be just as awkward and even suspicious. Whether on commission or not, I know that staff in this country can be overbearing to a fault. If I'm not straightforward with them, they would not leave me alone. If I'm straightforward with them, they may never leave me alone. I'm trapped.

If I had tried to fit in more, would this have happened? I had tried copying their mannerism before, albeit only briefly. On the one hand, it felt like re-learning how to ride a bike, clumsiness and all. On the other hand... It felt wrong. Where copying clothes is necessary, copying mannerisms is deceit. You wear clothes to fit the environment. Adapting to the local weather, following traditions, and cultural opinions on fashion are somewhat reasonable justifications to changing one's style. Mannerisms are something you grow into and develop from habit. There's a difference between playing soldier with children and faking to get a veterans' discount. I did not want to be a walking parody of the people around me.

Even without the mannerisms, I look the part and that can be a problem. My clothes are my first line of defence because they make people comfortable, think that we're the same. However, this also means that people would become comfortable enough to inspect me closely. Inspecting me closely means that they would start pointing out all that makes me unlike them. The more similar you are, the more vocal people would be about your differences. But if I don't look the part, they would decide I'm not one of them long before I even notice them. Either way, it never takes long for people to realize I am raised differently. It's a mistake to think someone like me could get away from this issue completely. I'm always set apart.

Even if I do respond in the local language, I'm doomed. She will know that I'm not like her. While the language is second nature to me, my tongue is molded differently than the locals. I can speak it and be understood easily but it marks me.

I was never ashamed of how different my tongue was. So long as I was understood by other speakers, it was fine. But the problem lies in the fact that my tongue has become a symbol of status. In fact, tongues touched by many nations have become popular in this country. Many of the rich and famous come from multicultural backgrounds which afforded them these tongues similar to mine. The country has acquired such a palate for these tongues that even those who never left their homeland try to cater to these new tastes. Is it wrong if the voices they are trying to copy were originally trying to copy them? I hear more of these foreign sounding tongues singing, preaching, and leading than the tongues I hear on this country's streets. They had manufactured their own tongues to appear touched by lands abroad, all to build followers.

My voice sounds rich to their ears. For some, my voice sounds like a demand. They think I use my voice to signify that I demand respect and will reward those who swear fealty. Many times I have been hounded in marketplaces by people begging to hear my voice. They want my tongue to feed their bellies with a simple "yes" to their demands. They follow the curves of my every word, like directions to their deepest dreams. They make offers like they want to make a trade for my tongue. Similarly, I worry this sales associate might try to wait on me like a servant if I speak. The thought unnerves me. I am horrified by what people would do for a voice.

I am not rich. I do not grant wishes. I do not want power over anyone. In reality, when I visit my family's homeland, I want to spend time with them. I seek to enrich my connection with my family. I want to help my family when I can. I want to learn and respect parts of my family I hardly ever see. A reunion necessitates only recognition, not demands. To demand power over any random person on the street is not the reason I go out, let alone hope for, in an area that could be considered another home away from home for me. I shudder to think of voices who use their marked status to use people, especially to take advantage of people in need.

I want to know the sales associate's tongue and I want her to know mine. I want to feel how both our tongues are the same, yet shaped differently. Where do our tongues contact comfortably? Where do we feel the tension that sets us apart?

What experiences have seasoned our tastes? I want to be able to exchange stories and jokes, not social mobility. I went off on my own so I could be part of the local crowd. Am I not allowed to be part of this country?

And yet, I still have not spoken because I have heard her tongue. Her expression is worried, like she's burdened by all the possibilities of why I haven't spoken. She studies me as much as I study her. We're both puzzled. Does she know those who have demanding voices? Does she worry about her own tongue? Is her uniform a line of defence? Is A/C a comfort for her or just something manufactured? What are we supposed to say?

Theory of Evolution

by Elizabeth Han

The kid's girlfriend phoned it in to his parents, who ran a red light at Bloor and Jarvis on the way to the viaduct.

I squint at the nurse's chicken scrawl, which indicates our patient pulled over and surveyed the barriers for an hour, considering how the middle school perched at the top of the hill meant, more likely than not, that some unsuspecting student would see his body fall, bounce, and break. One sentence under History of Present Illness proclaims EVOLUTION in all capitals, underlined twice, beside which she began to write something else, but blacked it out.

"Evolution?" I ask her outside the interview room of the Emergency Department. She makes a sign which seems to say *don't ask me*.

Since I've been back on rotation in psych emerg, it's become a cruel joke that she and I are always assigned the same call nights. Shoulder to shoulder, me in my physician's white coat and her in pink scrubs, we peer past netted glass at the boy's specs and buzzed haircut. Tiny embroidered dinosaurs march up and down the placket of his Oxford shirt, and the more he twists, the more they protest the shirt's seven mother-of-pearl buttons.

The boy's girlfriend, who's clutching his mother's hand while sizing up serrations in the ceiling of the waiting room, said he's taking anthropology at the University of Toronto and his favourite place on campus is Noranda, the earth sciences library, where he buries himself in geological journals lined with Latinate names and many-fingered phylogenies.

A switch on the wall will summon the guard if he starts to lose it. I'm certain he won't.

He's well aware, he tells me, when my interview follows that of the nurse, that cave people and dinosaurs were not contemporaneous. "But if they were, and if I were a caveman, I'd definitely have been eaten. Like, by a dinosaur. And it would be only right. I'm not fit to live in this world. Evolutionarily speaking."

"Thank you," I say.

When I come back out, the nurse, whose name is Lila, is waiting, chomping on a handful of cashews, eyes dancing, her tongue loosened.

"*Evolutionarily speaking*. I mean, who talks like that?" she says. "Do it or don't do it, but don't bring evolution into this crap."

She taps her pen against the glass, flushing when he startles bodily like a goldfish jostled by the cat. Four decades my senior, she must be close to retirement; she gets away with saying everything.

I crack my neck.

"Dr. Wong?" she prompts.

"He's a nice kid," I say.

I imagine him sitting in Noranda, at the round concourse, fortified by books, and the loamy soil smell that I know from the stacks and potted monstera and ficus. Before I graduated, I had shopped around U of T for the perfect library which I could call mine. Noranda with its greenery had ranked high on the list, but I settled on Laskin, the law library, where, for four years, I was safe from both other medical students and pre-meds taking enviro electives. It turns out that it is hard, but not impossible, to lone-wolf medicine. If you keep a packed schedule and politely skirt overtures to join intramural and subspecialty interest groups, people eventually stop asking. You gain a rep. When rumours about specialties tagged around the class, I was known as the Psych Gunner, which had a ring to it, like I was about to shoot up a school.

Ma didn't like my choice at all. Hearing that psych was five years of residency, she protested, "Do family. Easier. Only two." Ever since last July 1st, when my badge gained the sticker of Post-Graduate Year 1, she tells everyone that I'm a doctor, but not of the mind. She knows how to be proud of the former, but not of the latter. Back home in Halifax, where we moved from Hangzhou when I was four, I'm what's known as Chinese-famous. That means all the Chinese professors and scientists remember when I won the university mathematics contest, which gained me an invitation to the provincial camp, then the national camp, then the international camp, each step perfect paving stones to scholarships, an undergrad, a masters, and, finally, to my MD. At one of Ma's potlucks last Christmas, a little girl, the daughter of the new Chair of the Department of Mathematics, came up to the piano, where I'd been assigned to play carols and said, with shirred brows, "My dad misses you. Also, I'm supposed to ask you to do a duet." Her father waved at me from across the room. Waving back, I whispered, "Sit down, then. While he's still watching."

I shift to the rolling computer station. On the electronic medical record, I sketch out the boy's admission orders, which include twenty-four-hour observation at the rear of the ED, visual checks every fifteen minutes, and a pinch of lorazepam to put him to sleep.

Lila stands too close to me. She never looks over anyone's shoulder but mine.

"Yes?" I say.

"Maybe he's done for."

"No way."

"How do you figure?"

"Good support, heaps of insurance. He'll be fine," I say. Hell, I'd even feel confident leaving him in there with a blade, but that part I keep to myself.

She yawns and says offhandedly, "Okay. What about you?"

"Pardon? What about me?"

"Were *you* fine?" she says. "*Are* you fine?" Her pen touches the glass again and, this time, rests there. "Never mind."

I snap off listing the vitals. A red half-dome mole moves in an arc as Lila smiles. The hand which once passed me a paper cup and pointed to the bathroom with stalls but no main door, stripped of anything remotely sharp, readjusts the alarm on her lanyard. A breakaway design consisting of two parts, it isn't supposed to go off unless pulled with at least ten pounds of force, but the mechanism is flawed and we're always running after false wailings. The more she secures it, the more the grip of my own hands comes back to me, the cool dispassionate handle of the kitchen knife pressed to my arm, the soot-smelling air of the neighbour's grill through the screen door, Ma's scream, the blade sliding on the floor in a pool of my blood. I hate everything about this scene. Ma can't let it go either, even now, nearly a decade after my "accident." That day, the entire ambulance ride to the hospital, my arms wrapped in rags, she said it was taking all her restraint to keep from striking me in the presence of the medics. *Lang fei*, she muttered, end to end, *what a waste*. I've never been able to figure out if she meant the rags, the blood, or sixteen years of feeding, sheltering, and educating me. At psych reception, a woman with a half-dome mole met us, and later, she had stared from behind netted glass, recording my mental status exam in a binder marked WONG.

A width of silence slips between Lila and me while, down the hall, the vending machine thumps out a lukewarm Sprite, and the grim guard, pacing, cracks it open and slurps up a layer of foaming excess. I chew my tongue, acquainting myself with the taste. I really thought she forgot. Having something on me, she must have burned for weeks and waited for the perfect pretext, sneakier than the others who doused me and my cohort of fellow new residents with their digs while we pounced to prove ourselves.

My knuckles grow ghostly on the mouse; Lila's face is turned away. The kid's parents, like all the parents, addressed their pleas to me over her, unaware of the scarred earth on which they tread. Unconscious of salvos between newly-minted MDs just passing through and staff RNs who resented requiring their sign-off on a single regular-strength Tylenol.

I should let her win this one, I think. If I do, when I do, maybe we'll be able to share a laugh at the witching hours. I've seen Lila smoking out back, by the dumpsters, where we receive heavy shipping and exercise the more stable inpatients. Maybe I could take up my pack again, too.

I key in my access code to send off the orders. "Listen. Do you have the note? The parents are asking about it. They want it back."

"Here. Already scanned and uploaded," she says, drawing a folded sheet from her scrubs. "It's quite literary, you know. He has talent."

Mine is in an envelope I asked my mother to mail to me five months before, when I graduated with the letters after my name, to my new address, just south of Chinatown.

"How generous," I say. I watch her toss a cashew in the air and catch it in her mouth. I still use safety scissors to carve open packages. I own only plastic knives. "Would you like to tell them that?"

Lila slits her eyes. "You're up, Doc."

Of course I am. I touch my keycard to the scanner to enter the waiting area. The boy's mother is already standing, craning her neck, searching, and accidentally bumps her leg into the chair. I wish they would replace the cracked leather cushions, which are as uncomfortable as the day they dug into my skinny teenaged bottom.

There are twenty paces between us when our eyes meet. Her irises are neither the colour nor texture of Ma's but somehow the same. When she opens her mouth and closes it again, she doesn't make a sound.

How could he do this to me? How could she? They? Them? I can hear the cries. The accusations agitate off every wall in this place, every day, undifferentiated molecules striking one another down.

Like meaningless words, *pleistocene, holocene, anthropocene.*

One last time, I look towards the interview room, where the boy is still slumped, a fresh kill dragged back to the den. Bracketed by his times. The letter leaden in my pocket.

The woman lunges the rest of the way. I grip my pen and meet her in the middle.

POETRY

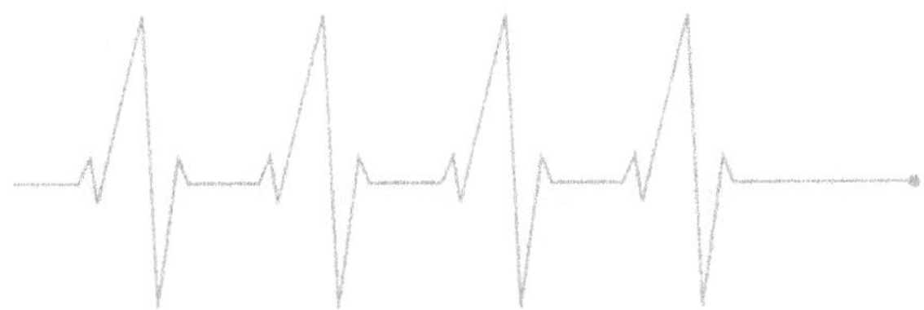

My Aunt
By Jim Wong-Chu

She raised me from a babe

and aged in her own time.

The years have taken her love

and cast them into my life.

She has seen eighty-three

years in this country

but none of my education.

She has shrunk

into herself

and I cannot follow.

We hug and kiss

awkwardly

but only on holidays

Is it understood

That I do love her?

25/3/78

THINGS YOU LEFT
BEHIND
BY MIHAN HAN

a hospital bed steeped in

ammonia currents of

stale urine

a tube of canesten straddling

the commode atop

a stack of unused diapers

fruit flies metastasizing from

browning bananas to

a half-empty bottle of lactulose

a walker curled like oriental

calligraphy against the couch in

a living room unreachable as China

a parchment of dust covering

Mahjong tiles, precious as tiger

bones, portending your fate

ghosts keening behind

glass walls, guarded by Buddha and

a jade elephant

the communists who seized

your property, leaving behind

rations of rice and flour, and

a little red book, to feed

3 hungry mouths

tobacco-stained fingers moulding

pork and chive

dumplings pregnant as

unspoken words of love

The Perpetual Foreigner

by Hana Kim

I am the sorrow of the perpetual outsider,

Carried on through centuries of pain.

Still hearing the echoes of souls once silenced,

From signs that read, "No Indians, Chinese, or dogs allowed."

The yellow peril never fades away,

A numbing pain that never ends.

Constantly sorted by skin-like breeds of dogs,

My identity forever in question.

Each morning I awake, believing I am at home,

But the blanket of prejudice soon reminds me I am not.

Discrimination and antagonism, a constant battle,

Every day I must shout, "I am not a virus!"

I stand tall, a symbol of strength and resilience,

But the weight of being a perpetual foreigner never leaves.

My voice a testament to the struggle and strife,

A reminder that our fight for equality never fades.

APRIL PARK

BY DOUGLAS SHIMIZU

Sun on my face, almost warm

But the air still bites

Not wanting to deny

Winter's slipping grip.

Few trees are still bare, asleep.

Crocuses bloom at their feet

Trying to tickle them awake

To enjoy the still weak sun shine.

Children's voices overpower

Busy birds beeping.

(Isn't it a school day?)

Is there still school these days?

My wardrobe has yet to feel the spring.

Flight jacket over fleece over Heattech

Fail to block today's gusts

Still chilling me, my coffee gone cold.

Shadow branches meander without destination,

No load, no flow to guide them.

No terrestrial master, they follow the sun,

Moving across the grass, minute by minute.

Once straight lines now curve over rock.

While wooden bends are straightened by illusion.

Their contortions further stretch as the hours lengthen,

Flat trees are now longer than they are high.

I, too, creep along the park bench

Chasing that sunny spot to light my reading.

A few more pages please before

I run out of wood.

MOTHER TONGUE
BY AMY GRACE LAM

1

At age four, I entered

a world completely foreign

to my Chinese roots

At the long dining room table

of my Argentinian babysitter's home

I sipped mate through a straw

used a fork to eat

fried pork chops and salad

and drank powdered chocolate milk

When we'd go out

she would fix my hair

I was like one of her daughters

high ponytail splashed with

Jean Naté

perfume on my head

And like a little bird

I followed along

Greeted people with

a kiss on the cheek

Listened to salsa music

blasting from the car

Dreamt about having

a gold chain necklace

in the shape of my name

In the Bronx, I was

allowed to exist

without the watchful eye

of a reserved Chinese mom

who said I was

a wild horse, mouth

too expressive and unbridled

for my own good

Muy rico,

sí,

más por favor

With a foreign language

on my tongue

I was practising how to fly

2

I practised speaking English

watching Barbara Walters

on 20/20

I watched her

calm collected manner

skilled at interviewing

notorious killers and

movie stars alike

She taught me

how to make small talk

about the latest NY Times story

present scientific data with objectivity

and confidently ask rich folks

about their legacy and contribution

to society

A friend once heard me

speak at a conference

"Wow, that was so white"

She stared at me in awe

I smiled back

feeling the tension in my jaw

I was still on camera

3

I learned French at age 14

when my family moved

to Montréal

My family was thrust

in the middle of a silent war

we knew nothing about

Like the time Mom

went to the post office

to mail a package

The teller spoke

only French

Mom pointed

with her fingers

and spoke

only English

All the bilingual clerks

just stared

Sometimes there was

a stalemate,

like in restaurants

"Qu'est-ce que

vous voudriez manger?"

"Smoked meat sandwich and poutine"

"Breuvage?"

"A coke"

"Merci"

"Thanks"

I thought a dictionary

would help

show I was eager

to learn and

make peace

like the time my teacher said

"six quarante-neuf"

I looked in the dictionary

but couldn't find

the word

I didn't even know

I had to look up

two words

"six"

"quarante-neuf"

In defeat

I whispered for help

from my classmates

They chuckled

"6-49?!"

"It's the Canadian lotto"

4

I thought I had forgotten

I was Chinese

after 14 years of marriage

to a white man

My mouth forgot

how to speak

Chinese, my taste buds

had grown accustomed

to swirling a fork to eat

spaghetti and meatballs

with red sauce

Though my lips

still missed

slurping chewy fat noodles

in vinegar soy sauce

with chopsticks and

a bowl to my face

Then one day

I found a song on YouTube

A woman in Cantonese

sang through the speakers

and gave me back

my childhood memories

The smell of stir-fry vegetables

garlic, ginger and hot oil

came wafting through the air

Eating dinner together

with wooden chopsticks

and porcelain bowls of hot rice

at our round table

I used to choreograph

elaborate ballet moves

on the yellow oriental rug

listening to Canto-pop

my unabashed dream

of being a Chinese superstar

I found a song on YouTube

Suddenly,

the song ended

and so did my memories

Instead I heard my mom's

impatient voice yelling

me back to reality

"Why are you crying

listening to this song?

You're not even Chinese."

5

As a child

I thought I could

erase away

my mother tongue

Swap it with

languages and adventures

that gave me freedom

to explore the world

to find myself

to feel lost

I thought my mouth

was a muscle

that with enough

practice would forget

about its past

Then at age 46

I read a book

of Chinese Medicine

and learned

The tongue

is the gateway

of the heart

It's curves and trills

how it touches

the roof of your palate

the tones it makes

as it sits in midair

in your mouth

They all remain

memories

of the heart

LANGUAGE CARDS
BY FRANCIS CHANG

I keep a faded box of Chinese language cards

on the bottom shelf of a basement bookcase.

The box is almost as old as me,

the cover once bright red,

now faded, pale, the beginnings of dusk.

The box holds over a thousand cards,

a thousand Chinese characters,

each card, still relatively crisp and white.

In the past fifty years, the box has been opened up

less than twenty times,

I'd guess.

The cards were created by

the Chinese language department of Yale.

Traditional Chinese characters on front,

Yale romanization on the back.

The paper for the cards

probably originated from forests in BC,

pulp sent to China to be pressed into cardboard,

printed and boxed, to be shipped

back to academic bookstores in

North America.

All available for anxious, conflicted,

Chinese Canadian, American

parents and students alike.

My mother got these cards for me –

was I ten or twelve?

was she feeling guilty

that I didn't seem Chinese at all?

The idea of the cards that if

you memorize them, master them,

you'll have enough for

a basic, every day vocabulary.

My mother left me with these cards,

to memorize, to figure out,

but language isn't an asynchronous activity.

It requires conversations,

acknowledgements of mistakes,

expressions of support.

I haven't been able to bring myself

to throw these cards away.

I still had hope that I would learn

how to speak,

how to connect

to something that, in theory,

is supposed to be part of me.

The cards are a museum piece now, outdated,

the traditional Chinese characters of Hong Kong

surely to be replaced

by the simplified characters of the Mainland,

sooner than later.

The cards are obsolete technologically

—nowadays kids use Google Translate.

That's how my son learned Chinese on his own.

If I don't get rid of these cards now,

my kids will toss them.

Will there be a moment

when they look at these cards,

along with the Chinese language texts

and children's books,

and they'll be reminded of

my attempts,

my failures,

my sentimentality.

ROCKY PLAYGROUND
BY VICTORIA SA

look at this rocky playground, where we scraped knees

to leave them bleeding, then outgrown the stagnant

navy blue and white uniforms, blown into different

directions, flying away-

until divine intervention brought us

back together, no longer naive, yet longing to be free

to do childish misfits and deeds, etching chalk graffiti

of our hopes and dreams, that remained temporarily, when

reality rained and washed them down the drain

and we remain playing nameless games on asphalt

terrain. sometimes taking the leap kills, twisting

life like juvenile ankles and uno reverses, arrays of aimless
green and red lights confuse feelings of yellows and blues. fear
breeds a barrier from traversing outside the track lines, stuck
hopscotching on a single foot into uncharted territory, returning
defeated to square one on this once familiar school property

bones can heal

don't let zealous desire burn to cast dregs
of shadows upon this school institution, consume
the bonfire, lay down your foundation, brick by brick, and
bounce back like a basketball. stick to goals like
decade-old bubblegum plastered on
these thick walls, and score

afterwards, remember to rest. lie down
in the tranquil shade, amidst half-empty bubble
tea drinks, honey butter chips and frosted Timbits
admire the radiant skies in this safe space, but

beware of incoming balls that could still hit
your face

CONTRASTS
BY DONNA SETO

The chipped wooden cane of my century-old grandmother

beats haphazardly against the damp asphalt drumming to

a history of broken dreams fossilized by grey-black gum

chewed by absent ancestors.

A moustached man on East Pender,

a has-been accountant with a southern Chinese accent

my grandmother once mistaken as her late husband,

hollers across the crowd of Sunday shoppers

    that his gai lan is fresher, greener,

        and crisper than his competitor on Keefer.

His calculated eyes full of adulterous ambitions,

   the slight upturn of his lips resembling a smile

      that women once swooned over during better times.

On sale, poh-poh, the man who is not my grandfather says.

   Bargain—

   Ninety-nine cents a pound.

      The man's village accent echoes down the paint-splattered

      street, sending pigeons flocking from frayed electric lines.

Hushed chatter

of forgotten rice patties and fermented fish

sundried on an old laundry line

above a charcoal fire

in a blackened hut

no different to the one

      my grandmother once called her home.

The tattered shoes on my grandmother's unbound feet shuffles

alongside graffitied walls and broken windows. Post-

apocalyptic scenes of a war-torn past made present except this

is not a war,

at least not the kind with guns and grenades.

Hungry tastebuds dance to the rhythm of fat

glistening on golden roast ducks

strung out on silver hooks in a butcher shop window on Gore,

    laminated with grease as thick as the layers of paint

        on its exterior.

The city donated paint to fix this graffiti problem, the butcher

tells my grandmother, breathing out a drawn-out sigh while

waving his cleaver, We suffer there, we suffer here.

    Who did I wrong in my past life?

My grandmother's cataract eyes squint

  at the shadows that flicker to the glow

    of a red paper lantern,

        while pale-skinned tourists watch the fat drip

        from carcasses

        like raindrops cascading to the ground

          from rooftops.

A hipster waltzes into the butcher shop,

in designer jeans he claims are from Value Village,

but he purchased on a whim from Nordstrom. Belly

full of foie gras served on heirloom sourdough, he

washes down with a

$7 oat milk latte,

while k-pop blasts from his thousand-dollar earbuds

as he snaps a photo

of my century-old grandmother.

Authentic china-doll poh-poh, the hipster says

as he shares the filtered snapshot with the world.

METEOROGRAPH
BY MARY ZHU

i knew my poh-poh

through my mother first—

a wordless woman

made cruel and callous by war,

by orphanage; undigested tones

chewed and spit out as lotus paste.

goldenrod teeth, appleseed eyes.

she put her memory down

in a burning bed

and never brought it back.

when i met her for the first and last time

she was the size of a yuan:

small yet patinated,

curled into the bent shape of my thumb.

my mother had her illness—the shape

of womanhood,

of motherhood,

of gunpowder silence. caught

in the crossfire as either the cynosure or

the catalyst, there was no use taking cover;

we exist

to be flammable.

"don't talk to her," my mother had warned me

during our thirteen-hour flight. "she doesn't remember

our faces. it's not worth the trouble."

but i didn't think trouble could look so lonely.

when i was too scared to sleep

i found her on the balcony tilted skywards

at the bruised stars.

trouble said nothing.

trouble brewed me piss-warm tea in the

qinghua porcelain she drank from everyday.

trouble lingered by my side until dawn

shadowed her planetary hands.

all mothers were their mothers

but maybe i was wrong for the first and last time.

that night,

trouble might've tried

to love me back.

All That I've Loved Most Dearly: for Helena Qi Hong

by Changming Yuan

When I die at another ant-like moment like this

No human crowds would gather to mourn my loss

Nor would anybody really notice my departure

Much less shed tears, even if because of the wind

Yet I am sure trees will shake off their leaves; horses

Will stampede, raindrops will taste somewhat salty

Hills & mountains will all murmur in a muted voice

Above all, Zhuhai will weep under sagging clouds

For it well knows there will be no more human soul

On this planet trying to connect with the city as far

As from beyond the Pacific, so closely & constantly

With its myriad spirited fingers caressing every

Synapse of the neighbourhood, the very building

Where you dwell, while poetry cannot help feeling

Empty as if its heart were hollowed by my absence

An Existence That We Can Call Home

by James Kim

Sitting quietly by the First Narrows

remembering The Lost Salmon-Run,

of the ravenous yearning for strength,

unaware of the consequences

that will devastate our community,

shattering the solace seen in the sea.

Rumbling throughout the city of glass.

Making space for something new, though

no one asked.

It was for the greater good, they said.

They lied

and we could not believe them

They sought power

to feed a starving greed

to gross and gluttonous excess.

Though they never thought

it came at a cost.

And they did not believe us.

We have only

  the memories,

    the stories,

      the truth to guide us,

ground us to an existence that we can call home.

When they tell us to never forget,

we must remind them

we have never forgotten.

We are taught by

  our parents,

    our peers,

      our people,

we could not trust those who break promises made.

Late Night Conversations with a Cockroach

by Amardeep Kaur

Shzzzzs, our little secret:

Many nights I slept with you on the Kowloon floor.

Then why would I be bothered by you

underneath the sinks and cracks

of my Regent Park neighbourhood?

In Tsim Sha Tsui, I'd wrap my little tired body,

tightly, in layered blankets—

my head and face fully covered.

My parents worried I would suffocate in sleep.

Little did they know of our deal:

me on this side of the fabric

you on the other side.

Sometimes I could tell you were nearby.

Should I peek up?

Your radio antennas and peripheral sight emitted

onto me   a telepathic sense.

But this will be our secret,

they won't understand it here.

When I lay awake on the sofa,

I feel close to your presence, I am not alone,

another creature crawls at night with me.

Now the Darwins have hoarded box stores. But they still

won't wear a face suit. Do they not know? If Covid doesn't

flatten soon, it will be you and not them eating all this food.

So I cannot help but ponder, if we reach such a moment,

would I, ever, attempt to boil you and make roach soup?

Humans may perish, and you may be the only ones left.

Make me a promise and crawl up to the nightdesk, punch

the keys with those long feelers, all that I could not write.

Let the world know of once a species that killed each other

extinct, but whose stories you carry now in your genes.

"Cockroaches, cockroaches", the policeman yells.

When Darwin created race

He threw you bottom of the table as well.

Now all wannabe Urban States

send blue troopers wearing terminator vests:

vapor, projectiles, barbed wire,

cannons, guns, bullets, tasers, tanks.

Blood drips, eyes burnt,

throats squeezed.

Skin, feelers kicked and ripped.

But we are roaches:

black, brown, red, yellow

opaque and transparent.

No traps, nor nukes, no law

can change our breeding truth.

During lunch, we strike

flowing with water, thrive.

Gas, retreat. Disaster, adapt.

Along pipes, merge

with night, we fly.

Serpents, birds, insects, and now

hybrid human selves

I'm Jealous of the Students at Seoul International

by Justin Timbol

I'm jealous of the students

at Seoul International

and how they practice

second languages, the way

they write and unwrite poems

in English

to learn how

they fit inside the words.

Each one neatly rested

inside individual folds

of the cloud,

the prettiest ones

rounded up,

waiting for the moment

night rolls over

and their poems

join a Western morning.

In the Korean school system,

rejection from literary journals

comes softened by the promise

of extra credit. Google auto-fills

my typing because the algorithm

knows my thoughts before I do,

knows I will always find myself

trying to fill the same spaces

in the sky. I am still trying

to understand where I fit

inside this language

that is my one and only.

In the Zoom meeting,

I raise a virtual hand,

not to ask any question

just to touch the face

of someone who has helped me

navigate this vastness that is

my being.

About the Authors

Rachel Abelinde

Rachel Abelinde is a Filipino lawyer based in Manila.

———

Francis Chang

Francis Chang is a Chinese Canadian who was born in Tokyo, grew up in Vancouver, worked in Hong Kong and recently returned to Vancouver with his family. Francis practised law for over 25 years, including 14 years working for The Walt Disney Company and Twenty-First Century Fox. In the last few years, Francis has been involved with the NY Writers Coalition, poetry, short stories and creative non-fiction to explore questions of filial duty versus love, facts versus conclusions and Western versus Asian views of the world.

———

Yang Changming

Yuan Changming grew up in an isolated village and began to learn the English alphabet in Shanghai at age 19. With a Canadian PhD in English, Yuan edits *Poetry Pacific* with Allen Yuan in Vancouver. Credits include 12 Pushcart nominations, 15 collections & appearances in *Best of the Best Canadian Poetry (2008-17)*, *BestNewPoemsOnline* & *Poetry Daily*, among 2019 others, across 49 countries. Yuan was a poetry judge for Canada's 2021 National Magazine Awards. Early in 2022, Yuan began writing and publishing fiction.

————

Ling Ge Chen

Ling Ge studies creative writing and works as a statistician in Toronto. She is a graduate of The Writer's Studio at Simon Fraser University. In her literary work, she explores a combination of Eastern metaphysics and the English language's plasticity. As a first-generation Chinese immigrant, she writes to promote diversity and inclusion. She has had short stories published in *The Spadina Literary Review* and *Ricepaper*. Her first published short story was nominated for The 2020 Pushcart Literary Prize. Her poems have appeared in *Ribbons, Wales Haiku Journal, The Rising Phoenix Review*, and are forthcoming in *emerge 23*.

————

Carla Crujido

Carla Crujido is the author of the short story collection, *The Strange Beautiful*, as well as the chapbook, *The Bear*. She is also the co-editor of the anthology, *Nonwhite and Woman: 131*

Micro Essays on Being in the World. Her work has appeared in *Ricepaper Magazine, Tinfish Press, Yellow Medicine Review, Crazyhorse,* and elsewhere. Carla is the Nonfiction Editor at *River Styx Magazine,* and holds an MFA in Creative Writing from the Institute of American Indian Arts. She lives in the Pacific Northwest.

———

Garry Engkent

Garry Engkent, a Chinese-Canadian, has a Ph.D. and taught at various universities and colleges for over 30 years. He co-authored three texts*: Groundwork: Writing Skills to Build On; Fiction/Non-Fiction: A Reader and Rhetoric; and Essay: Do's and Don'ts. 3rd ed.* His fictional stories have appeared in *Exile, Many-Mouthed Birds, Emerge, and Ricepaper Magazine.* Most stories have a Chinese immigrant slant: "Why My Mother Can't Speak English","Eggroll", and "Rabbit". His recent published foray into horror is "I, Zombie: A Different Point of View,""We Aren't Bad Guys," and "Merci."

———

Marcel Goh

Marcel Goh was born in Singapore, grew up in Leduc, Alberta, and is currently pursuing a Ph.D. in combinatorics at McGill University. His short fiction has appeared in the *Prairie Journal* and *Existere.*

———

Elizabeth Han

Elizabeth Han is a Newfoundland-raised, British Columbia-based physician and writer. She is a graduate of the Doctor of Medicine (M.D.) program from the University of Toronto and practices family medicine in Chilliwack, BC. Her short fiction has recently appeared in *Sine Theta, The Windsor Review,* and *Ricepaper.* Connect with her at elizabethhan.com and on Twitter @effyhan.

———

Mihan Han

Mihan Han was born in Mudanjiang, China. As a child, he immigrated with his parents, first to the United States before settling in Canada. An unabashed gamer, nerd, and amateur musician, he lives in Toronto, Ontario and practices Internal Medicine in Scarborough. His poetry has appeared in *Ricepaper Magazine, Juniper, Modern Haiku, Frogpond,* and others. He can be found on Twitter: @MrMihanHan.

———

Riley-Grace Huggins

Riley-Grace Avelina Huggins is the author of the story "Heritage." Her writing has been published in *Ricepaper Magazine* and *In Her Space Journal.* She is a graduate of Texas Woman's University, where she studied English Literature, History, and Journalism. She lives in Fort Worth, Texas.

———

Amardeep Kaur

Amardeep Kaur is a Hongkonger and presently lives in Tkaronto. She holds a PhD in Geography and a graduate diploma in Asian Studies from York University. Kaur is a sessional lecturer at University of Toronto where she teaches Canada-Hong Kong Migration. When not writing or teaching, she likes walking and drinking endless cups of cha.

Hana Kim

Hana Kim, a first-gen Korean Canadian, is the Director of the East Asian Library at the University of Toronto. Formerly Head at the Asian Library at the University of British Columbia (UBC), her publications focus on Asian Canadian heritage and library studies. Hana initiated the Korean Canadian Heritage Archives Project in 2009 with UBC. She has been honoured with the 2018 Korean Canadian Heritage Award, the 2008 Harvard Sunshik Min Prize for poetry translation, and the Korea Times 41st Modern Korean Literature Translation Award for Poetry. Hana translated "Love is the Pain of Feverish Flowers" (2016) and edited *Asian Canadian Voices: Facets of Diversity* (2022).

James Kim

James Kim is a Korean-American art therapist and poet living in what is now known as Canada. After moving to Canada to attend a graduate program in art therapy, he continued to write and live in the country. When they're not writing or being an art therapist, James enjoys playing video games, reading books, and watching movies or television. He is so grateful for the opportunity to have their poetry be written and read alongside other amazing poets and poems. Thank you for reading his and the many other wonderful poems that were included! (IG: @james00poetry)

———

Amy Grace Lam

Amy Grace Lam (she/they) is a Chinese Canadian-American writer-performer-healer creating immersive experiences for transformation and expansion. Amy explores the convergence of the spiritual, natural and physical worlds for bringing renewed awareness and consciousness of life to humanity. Amy's writings are featured in *Asian Week, Asian American Literary Review, Feministing.com, Marsh Hawk Review, Moyama Press, Pochino Press, Ricepaper* and *VONA*. She is currently working on *Out of the Box*, an experimental VR play (2021 San Francisco Arts Commission grantee). Amy develops innovative community mental health programs with immigrant/refugee organizations and is founder of Vibrational Energy Wellness. She resides with her family in San Francisco, CA, USA.

———

Wayne Mok

Wayne Mok is a writer originally from Hong Kong, now based in Sydney, Australia.

———

Sambriddhi Nepal

Sambriddhi Nepal (she/her) is a Nepali settler living on unceded Coast Salish Territories in what is now Vancouver BC. She works at an environmental organization by day and writes creative non-fiction and children's books when everyone in her household has gone to bed.

Victoria Sa

Victoria Sa (she/her) is a Burmese-Karen Canadian writer and poet from Toronto, ON. She graduated from York University with a BA in English and Creative Writing. Her favourite genres to write are contemporary, romance, and comedy. Focusing on self-identity, she hopes to share more of the Burmese-Karen culture in her work. When she is not writing, Victoria can be found binging Asian dramas, reading novels, or starting DIY projects at home. Connect with her on vrssstudios.wixsite.com, or on IG as @thelitvicblog.

Donna Seto

Donna Seto (she/her) is a Vancouver-based writer, academic and self-taught artist who was once told that art wouldn't get her anywhere. She is drawn to urban settings, marginalized communities, layered histories, and the complexity of memory. Donna is currently working on an illustrated history book on Vancouver's Chinatown, a novel, and a book of essays.

Douglas Shimizu

Douglas is a multi-media artist from Vancouver. He grew up in the Powell Street Japantown area when there still was a Japantown. After finishing UBC, he lived in Japan for a decade, teaching and studying linguistics. After returning to Vancouver, he has been feeding his curiosity by writing, drawing, painting and playing music.

Klaus Tan

Klaus Tan is a professional writer trained in Literature, Psychology, and Philosophy. He's spent much of his life studying Europe and Asia by book and by foot, learning about people and his own placement in the world. Much of his writing reflects such experience, leaving room for different perspectives from around the globe. His works include a variety of genres within Fiction, as well as Non-Fiction journalism work archiving the plight of minority groups in North America, Europe, and Asia. Born and raised in Canada, Tan is of mixed Filipino and Chinese descent with a smattering of European genes.

Kenneth Tanemura

Kenneth Tanemura has an MFA in Creative Writing from Purdue University. His stories have appeared in *The Iowa Review*, *Every Day Fiction*, *Fractured Literary*, *Atticus Review* and elsewhere.

Justin Timbol

Justin Timbol is a Filipino writer from Mississauga, ON. His work has been longlisted for the CBC Poetry Prize (2021) and shortlisted for CV2's Foster Poetry Prize (2021). Poems of his can be found most recently in *Vallum* and *Contemporary Verse 2,* among others, and will be forthcoming in *THIS Magazine.* He recently graduated from the Humber School for Writers.

———

Saya Watanabe

Saya Watanabe's second short story titled *"Nishi,"* was long listed for the CBC Short Story Prize in 2021. She received a Bachelor of Arts in English from SFU where she was the recipient of two creative writing awards. Her writing explores themes of identity, diaspora, and relationships. She currently resides and works as an educator in Vancouver, BC. Her poems and short stories have been published in *Ricepaper magazine, PRISM international,* and *The New Quarterly.*

———

Mary Zhu

Mary Zhu (she/they) is a poet based in British Columbia. A few of her previous works have been published in The Literary Canteen. When she is not in the process of writing, which includes a lot of self-imposed isolation, they can be found daydreaming in the middle of the produce section, or on Instagram @mewchive.

About the Team

Allan Cho - Editor

Allan Cho is an academic librarian at the University of British Columbia and an instructor at the University of the Fraser Valley. Allan is actively engaged in a number of initiatives in the community and has served on the board of the Asian Canadian Writers' Workshop Society (ACWW), Chinese Canadian Historical Society of British Columbia (CCHSBC) and Vancouver Asian Heritage Month Society (VAHMS). He has written for the *Georgia Straight, Diverse Magazine,* and *Ricepaper.* His fiction has appeared in the anthologies, *The Strangers* and *Eating Stories: A Chinese Canadian and Aboriginal Potluck.*

———

JF Garrard - Editor

JF Garrard is an award winning speculative fiction writer, editor, publisher and host of *The Artsy Raven* podcast about writing and publishing. She is the President of Dark Helix Press, serves as the President for the Canadian Authors Association's Toronto Branch, and Deputy Editor for *Ricepaper Magazine.* Her portfolio of books and short fiction is listed on jfgarrard.com and you can find her on Twitter, Instagram, TikTok, Youtube @jfgarrard.

Sophie Munk - Acquisitions Editor

Sophie is a graduate from McGill University, where she majored in international development and history. She is currently a coordinator at PCHC-MoM Society, one of ACWW's partner organizations. She has a background in community based initiatives, research, and service. She is planning on pursuing a career focusing on the relationship between culture and health governance in an international context.

Phoebe An Lee - copy editor

Phoebe An Lee has written and edited for various media, such as newspapers, marketing collateral, project proposals and other corporate communications materials. Her real love, however, is writing martial arts fantasy, where she can let her imagination roam free. As a third culture kid growing up Filipino-Chinese-Canadian and living in various countries in her young adult life, she is inspired by her cultural upbringing and committed to advancing diversity in literature. She is also an executive of the Canadian Authors Association in Toronto, holding the position of Treasurer and Programmer, and a literary editor for *Ricepaper Magazine*. She can be found at: https://www.phoebe-an-lee.com/

Chio Gonzalez - cover designer

Chio Gonzalez works in communications in the post-secondary sector. With a background in photography, graphic design, and copywriting, he enjoys the process of developing communications solutions that are grounded, thoughtful, and resonant. Taking inspiration from his identity as a Filipino immigrant, he strives to approach communications and other related disciplines in an emphatic and inclusive manner. In his free time, Chio enjoys taking pictures in and around Vancouver, equipped with good coffee and food. www.chiogonzalez.com

———

KATYA ROXAS - ILLUSTRATOR

Katya Roxas is an award-winning multimedia designer, post-secondary communicator, and illustrator. Her work has been featured in CBC Life, *The Walrus, Chatelaine Magazine,* BC Historical Foundation, and the National Forum on Anti-Asian Racism. Katya's personal work reflects her love for food, travel, and multiculturalism. katyaroxas.com

About Ricepaper

Ricepaper first began as a newsletter for the Asian Canadian Writers' Workshop (ACWW)—eight pages which were photocopied back-to-back and stapled together. It was a way for ACWW members to communicate with each other as well as celebrate individual successes. ACWW, a non-profit organization, continues to operate and publish *Ricepaper* today. From these humble beginnings, *Ricepaper* became a quarterly magazine that was distributed coast-to-coast, featuring new voices emerging from the Asian Canadian arts and literary community. With advancements in technology, *Ricepaper* then moved online, thus affording writers a wider audience and richer medium to deliver ideas.

Ricepaper publishes anthologies, novels, and other full-length works while maintaining its existing web presence. Therefore, *Ricepaper* continues to be the longest running literary organization of its kind with an Asian Canadian perspective.

Visit us at ricepapermagazine.ca to read the latest stories and Asian culture content. We are constantly looking for new voices!

About Dark Helix Press

Dark Helix Press is an independent publisher based in Toronto, specializing in speculative fiction, non-fiction, and children's books. Founded with the goal of providing diverse and innovative voices in the literary world, the press focuses on stories that explore unique perspectives, often blending genres to create thought-provoking and engaging narratives.

With a commitment to supporting underrepresented authors, Dark Helix Press has built a reputation for publishing works that challenge conventions and encourage readers to expand their imaginations. The press's catalog includes a range of titles that appeal to readers of all ages, from captivating speculative tales to insightful non-fiction and charming children's books.

Visit us at darkhelixpress.com.